Mary H. Collins

Deception

AF210301

Mary H. Collins

Deception

A Novel

JustFiction Edition

Impressum/Imprint (nur für Deutschland/only for Germany)
Bibliografische Information der Deutschen Nationalbibliothek: Die Deutsche Nationalbibliothek verzeichnet diese Publikation in der Deutschen Nationalbibliografie; detaillierte bibliografische Daten sind im Internet über http://dnb.d-nb.de abrufbar.

Coverbild: www.ingimage.com

Verlag: JustFiction! Edition ist ein Imprint der
LAP LAMBERT Academic Publishing GmbH & Co. KG
Heinrich-Böcking-Str. 6-8, 66121 Saarbrücken, Deutschland
Telefon +49 681 37 20 310, Telefax +49 681 37 20 310-9
Email: info@justfiction-edition.com

Herstellung in Deutschland:
Schaltungsdienst Lange o.H.G., Berlin
Books on Demand GmbH, Norderstedt
Reha GmbH, Saarbrücken
Amazon Distribution GmbH, Leipzig
ISBN: 978-3-8454-4505-2

Imprint (only for USA, GB)
Bibliographic information published by the Deutsche Nationalbibliothek: The Deutsche Nationalbibliothek lists this publication in the Deutsche Nationalbibliografie; detailed bibliographic data are available in the Internet at http://dnb.d-nb.de.

Cover image: www.ingimage.com

Publisher: JustFiction! Edition
is an imprint of the publishing house
LAP LAMBERT Academic Publishing GmbH & Co. KG
Heinrich-Böcking-Str. 6-8, 66121 Saarbrücken, Germany
Phone +49 681 37 20 310, Fax +49 681 37 20 310-9
Email: info@justfiction-edition.com

Printed in the U.S.A.
Printed in the U.K. by (see last page)
ISBN: 978-3-8454-4505-2

Chapter One

Sheets lay in a heap on the floor. Jillian picked up the wrinkled dress, pulling it over her head. She had to get home before Cyndi realized she'd spent the night with Travis.

"I hope I can get inside the house before the neighbors see me wearing this dress. They'll know I've been out all night," Jillian said, kissing Travis goodbye.

"They'd be envious." He nibbled her neck, pulling her back down onto the bed. "Can't you stay a little longer?"

"No, as much as I'd love to come back to bed, I've got to get home before Suzette gets up. She can't know we've been together all night."

"Why not…? She'll soon see me around a lot more often."

"Does that mean you want to marry me?"

"I told you I'm moving my business from Paris to New York so I can be with you. What do you think that means?"

"Speaking of Paris, you'd better get up and dress or you'll miss your flight." She hated the way he evaded her question.

"Are you sure you don't want me to drop you off at your place?"

"No thanks, I've already called a cab. I'll see you soon, love you." It took all her will power to walk out of his hotel room. Since losing her husband, thirteen years earlier, Jillian hadn't felt this passionate with anyone until meeting Travis.

Her cell phone rang as she stepped into the cab. The display read *Melody Mendoza*, her best friend since college.

"Hi Mel, It's good to hear from you. I've got great news."

"What…Are you selling your late husband's business and retiring?"

"No, I've met a man." Jillian didn't want to retire. The business kept Thomas' memory alive. Now that she'd met Travis, she might change her mind.

"It's about time. I hope you like him more than the previous ones you've been out with."

"I think he's the one. His name is Travis Johnson, and he owns a transport company in Paris. I met him when he came to New York on business. He asked me out to dinner and we've been seeing each other ever since." Jillian talked fast, trying to tell her friend everything about this wonderful man. "Always before when a man tried to get passionate with me, I'd turn cold inside, but I can't get enough of Travis. I want to spend every waking hour with him." She hoped the cabbie couldn't hear her conversation, but then…what the hell? He'd probably heard worse.

"I've gotta beep, call you back later." Melody hung up before Jillian could tell her about the wonderful night she'd spent with Travis.

"That'll be twenty-two dollars Ma'am." The cab driver pulled to the curb, turned off the meter, and stopped the car.

"Keep the change." She handed him several bills, rushed inside, and ran upstairs to her bedroom.

"Mom is that you?" Suzette called from her room.

"Yes dear, I overslept; you'll have to make your own breakfast."

"Did I hear you just come in?"

"Oh no honey, I went outside to get the paper. That darn paperboy threw it over in the neighbor's yard again." She hated lying to her daughter, but seems lately she did it often.

Jillian got into the hot shower, groaning when she saw the passion marks on her breast from his fondling and kisses. Just thinking of him made her blood run hot. She could hardly wait to be in his bed again.

"Mom, hurry up, I need to get in there," Suzette called, knocking on the bathroom door.

"Can't you use the shower downstairs?"

"No, my make-up is in this one. You're taking too long."

"Ok, I'll be right out." Jillian turned off the water, wrapped herself in a towel, and unlocked the door. "It's all yours."

"Thanks Mom, I don't want to be late for school."

"You have plenty of time. It's only a little after seven." Jillian knew she couldn't argue with her. She took her punctuality after her father as well as her looks.

"Did Josh ask you to the prom?"

"No, I'm going with Justin Henley."

"I'm sorry dear; I know how much you wanted Josh to ask you." Jillian knew Suzette had been in love with Josh since junior high. They'd always gone to the movies together. The day he took Wendy Jones, it broke Suzette's heart. Although she'd dated other boys, she never got over Josh. "I'm going to the office early today. We have a meeting with stockholders. I'm thinking I might sell." Jillian hurried to the kitchen, she at least had time for a cup of coffee with her daughter.

Twenty minutes later, Suzette walked into the kitchen, dressed in her favorite jeans and sweater.

"How'd the fundraiser go last night?" She poured a cup of coffee, took a sip, and made a face.

"Excuse me…? Oh the fundraiser…uh...it went well." She couldn't tell her daughter she'd spent the night at the Hyatt Regency making wild, passionate, love until three in the morning.

"What time did you get home?" Suzette picked up the paper and flopped down on a bar stool.

"Around Midnight…I think. We went for coffee afterwards. Travis wanted to talk to me about something."

"What about…? Did he ask you to marry him?"

"Not yet, but he's getting close." She could hardly believe her little girl would graduate high school in a few weeks. Seems only yesterday she'd changed her diaper and rocked her to sleep.

"I hope so. I know you've been lonely since Dad died. I have to run…see you later." Suzette folded the paper back the way she'd found it. Walking over to where her mother sat, she leaned over, kissing her on the cheek.

"Be careful and don't text while driving." She watched her daughter pull out of the driveway. Suzette drove safely, yet as a mother, Jillian worried.

She finished getting dressed and drove the few miles to Bradford Advertising, where she held the position as CEO.

"Good morning Mrs. Bradford," Sara, her secretary, said as she walked into her office. "I rescheduled your hair appointment for four thirty today."

"Thank you Sara. I don't know what I'd do without you." Unlike most of Thomas' personal staff, Sara stayed after his death thirteen years earlier.

"I remember what a hard time Mr. Bradford had building this company from the ground up. I promised him I'd stay with him. I loved him like a son." A tear formed in the elderly woman's eye.

"And he felt the same about you. If not for you, I dread to think what Thomas would've done." Jillian remembered the early years when the company struggled as a baby in a giant corporate world. In spite of the offers Thomas had from others to buy the struggling company, he had faith that brought his business to the very top. Now Bradford Advertisements employed over a thousand people, and had offices in five major cities.

"I don't know how much longer I can work. You know I'm no spring chicken. I'll soon be sixty-five. I think you should sell out and move to a tropical island with that sexy man you're seeing. He's got plenty of money, and with your money, you'd have the life most of us dream of." Sara laughed and winked at Jillian.

"I've given it some thought, but we'll see what happens." Thomas left her plenty of money and a beautiful home worth a half million dollars or more. She didn't work out of necessity, but the need for something to help ease the pain of her loss.

Her cell phone rang. Looking at the display she smiled.

"Hello Baby." She held her hand over the speaker and looked at Sara. "Excuse me please."

"Hey Teddy Bear, just wanted to call and say I miss you," Travis said in his sexiest voice. He'd nicknamed her 'Teddy Bear' on their second date, and never called her anything else.

"I miss you too, and I'm counting the hours until you get back to me." She'd grown accustomed to his frequent business trips to Paris in the months they'd dated.

"I'll finish up my business here and should be back before you know it. I love you. See you soon."

Before Jillian hung up, Melody beeped in.

"Hi Jill, what I called to tell you earlier is I'll be down that way next month. I thought we might get together for a girl's night out. It's been forever since I've seen you." Melody's job as a world renowned interior designer kept her on the go. They did well to get together once or twice a year.

"That sounds great. You'll get to meet Travis."

"I want to know more about this mystery man you've found."

"Like me, he's been married, but lost his wife in an automobile accident. She lost control of her car when the brakes failed, sending her swerving off the side of a cliff. She died instantly. He cried when telling me the story. He said until meeting me he had no hope for the future."

"If I didn't know you better, I'd be skeptical of him, he sounds too good to be true."

"He's a great deal like Thomas. The only difference in him and my late husband is Travis shies away from crowds. If I didn't know better I'd think he's hiding something." She laughed.

"Be careful girlfriend, there's a lot of cons out there, got a beep…talk to you later."

Chapter Two

Suzette sat at the kitchen counter with her laptop open.

"I didn't expect you home this early on a Friday," Jillian said. "I thought you'd be at the mall, hanging out with friends."

"Actually Mom, I'm spending the weekend with Tara. Her mother is taking us shopping for prom dresses tomorrow and Sunday we're hiking. I wanted to finish this paper for English first."

"That's wonderful dear, have fun." Of course, this gave Jillian the opportunity for another wonderful, passion filled night with Travis.

"By the way…did Travis reach you? He called here for you."

"Yes, he returned from his trip earlier than anticipated. He's taking me to dinner tonight."

"I'm glad you have plans. I hate thinking of you sitting in this house alone all weekend." Suzette picked up her keys, heading for the door.

"Be careful dear." Jillian closed the door behind her, turned and hurried upstairs. She had to get dressed for her date.

An hour later the doorbell rang. Jillian rushed to answer it.

"You look stunning. I love your hair." Travis wheeled her around, checking out the back of her new shorter cut.

"You looked great as well." She moved into his arms, her pulse racing as he nuzzled her neck.

"I can't wait to get you alone." His hands roamed her body. His lips met hers'.

"I'm free for the entire weekend," she whispered between kisses.

"We'd better get going, another kiss like that and we'll never make it past the bedroom."

"Let me grab my jacket."

"Hurry, our reservation is for seven. I'll have to drive like hell to make it." And he did. Twenty minutes later they arrived at the Bryant Park Hotel.

Walking into the crowded dining room, Jillian felt eyes following them. They made the perfect couple. When Travis first came to New York, girls ranging in ages twenty-five to fifty competed for his affections. This being a small suburb, eligible bachelors stood out like a sore thumb. Travis left many broken hearts when he began dating Jillian Bradford.

"I'm the envy of every woman in the room," she whispered to Travis.

"Did you talk to Suzette about the Paris trip?" He took her hand in his.

"I haven't had time yet, but I plan to tell her Monday."

"We'll be there only a week, maybe two. I'd like very much for you to go."

"I'd love to go to Paris. I've been there once, and always wanted to return." Thoughts of Thomas came to mind, but this time it didn't hurt. Maybe Travis planned to propose while in Paris. She just knew he was getting close to popping the question.

"Do you want to stay at my condo tonight or your place?" Travis brought her thoughts back to the present.

"Let's stay at my place. Suzette's not home."

They rushed through dinner, not even having dessert.

"I'm ready to go home and relax. How about you…?" He asked, squeezing her thigh under the table, before his fingers found their way all the way to her lacy thong.

"I'll beat you to the car." She stood up, grabbing her purse while he paid the check.

"I don't know how Suzette will take the news of me going to Paris for a week without her. The only time she and I have been apart is when she went to Bible camp, except on the nights she spends at Tara's." Jillian said on the way home.

"It's not like she's a baby," Travis pointed out. "She's an adult now. She'll be eighteen in a few months. It'll be good for her to fend for herself for a few days. Maybe it'd teach her to appreciate the life she has."

"After her father died, I over indulged her out of sympathy. Nevertheless, she turned out to be a good girl. I'm exceedingly proud of her."

"Let's concentrate on the plans I have for us tonight, and forget everything else," Travis said, pulling into the driveway of Jillian's house.

"I hope those plans include having champagne in the Jacuzzi." Jillian said, taking his hand.

"You read my mind. I'll grab the champagne while you get the glasses."

"You got it." She took two champagne goblets from the cabinet and headed for the stairs.

"Let's get out of these clothes," Travis said, coming up behind her to unzip her dress.

She assisted him in getting her clothes off and stepped into the hot tub of bubbles. He followed her.

"I need to go shopping before going to Paris. There are a few things I need to pick up."

"Let's talk about it later. My mind is on other things at the moment." He pulled her onto his lap and his lips covered hers. Two hours later, they got out of the tub and he carried her to bed.

Waking up hours later amongst tangled sheets, she lay nude, thinking of what had taken place. She'd never been loved so completely, even with Thomas. As she rolled over to get closer to Travis, he folded her into his arms and they melted together.

****

All day Monday, Jillian considered ways of telling Suzette about the trip to Paris. Taking off work early, she stopped at the supermarket to buy her daughter's favorite foods. She'd barely finished setting the table when she heard a car pull into the drive way.

"Ummm…something smells good," Suzette said walking through the door.

"It's baked Pollock. I've prepared your favorite dessert too. Let's eat before it gets cold." Jillian wanted to have dinner with her and talk about the trip to Paris.

"What's the occasion?" Suzette asked between bites.

"I want to tell you that Travis invited me to go to Paris with him." She waited for the response.

"When…? I hope you'll wait until after the prom, it's only another week."

"Yes dear, I wouldn't go away before your senior prom, and of course I'll be at your graduation. We plan to leave at the end of this month."

"Sure Mom, go ahead and have fun. Stay as long as you like. I'll be fine."

"Do you have plans for the summer? Maybe you'd like to go to Paris as well."

"Thanks for asking, but yes Mom, I plan to take a summer job at the youth camp. Coach Haynes says they need two part-time life guards. Tara and I applied for the positions."

Suzette's cell phone rang.

"I'm going on the back porch Mom." Like most teenagers, Suzette wanted her privacy.

After loading the dishwasher, Jillian poured boiling water over two tea bags. She carried the cups of chamomile tea to the porch. It'd been months since she'd enjoyed looking at the stars with Suzette.

"Thanks Mom, but I'm still on the phone. May I have some privacy please?"

8

"Yes you may. Good night. I'm going to bed." After the weekend she'd had with Travis, Jillian actually needed the rest anyway.

****

"Mom, Are you awake?" Suzette stood at the bedroom door.

"I am now. What time is it?"

"Its seven forty-five. I'm leaving for school."

"I'm sorry I overslept. Drive carefully, see you later." The weekend exhausted her. She'd just dozed back off when the phone rang.

"Hello."

"Good morning Teddy Bear. I called to tell you I had a wonderful weekend."

"Me too, but I'm re-thinking going to Paris. With Suzette's graduation and all…"

"You have to go. I've reserved a luxurious room with a magnificent view."

"I'll think about it and let you know by tomorrow night." It devastated her to think of not going. It could be the only chance she'd ever have to go there with Travis. But then, she felt Suzann needed her. Of course she wouldn't admit it.

"Next weekend I'd like for you and Suzette to come stay at my condo on the beach. I have three bedrooms, so there's plenty of room. It'll give Suzette a chance to get to know me better."

"That'd be great!" Jillian said, yet when she told Suzette about it, her daughter declined.

"I've already made plans to go to the movies Saturday night with the youth group. On Sunday, after church Tara and I are going to a birthday party at Julie Miller's house. You should go to the beach and have fun Mom, you deserve it."

Truthfully, Jillian didn't mind that her daughter had other plans.

Chapter Three

The weekend started off great, the early vacationers took advantage of the cool air and the white sand beach. This used to be Jillian's favorite place to come. She didn't tell Travis, but this is where she and Thomas started their honeymoon. They'd stayed two days here and then on to Mexico by plane. Not exactly, the way they planned it, but their plane was delayed due to a sudden thunderstorm brewing in the Atlantic. They'd spent two whole days here, lying in bed in a luxurious hotel room and making love under the stars on the deserted beach at three in the morning.

"A penny for your thoughts," Travis said, sitting her bags down in front of the sofa.

"I'm thinking about how much fun we'll have this weekend," she said without hesitating.

"You're right Teddy Bear; we're going to make some long term memories. What do you want to do first?"

"Why don't we take a walk on the beach before lunch?"

"I had something else in mind." He took her hand, leading her into the bedroom.

Being at his condominium set the mood for Jillian to show Travis what a wonderful wife she'd be.

"Let me put this food into the fridge before it spoils." They'd picked up food and wine at the supermarket before driving the two hours to the ocean. As it turned out they didn't get out of bed for the rest of the day, except to eat a late dinner.

"This Lasagna is delicious. I didn't realize you were such a great cook?"

"It's an old family recipe." Actually she'd found it online.

After a couple more rounds of lovemaking, they slept soundly.

"Maybe we can take that walk on the beach today," Travis said, stretching as he climbed out of bed.

"Yes, that'd be nice. I'll beat you to the shower." They ran, getting there at the same time.

"Looks like we'll be sharing," Travis said, turning on the water. "I'll scrub your back if you'll scrub mine."

****

Sifting the white sand between their toes, they walked up the beach, considering where to have breakfast.

"There's a pancake restaurant a few more blocks," Travis said. "They make the best blueberry pancakes I've ever eaten."

"That sounds great. I've worked up a good appetite."

Travis told the truth about the blueberry pancakes. They were the best she'd ever had.

"I'll remember this place incase I'm ever here again." Jillian stabbed her fork into the remaining bite of pancake.

"I'm sure you'll be back dozens of times. This is only the beginning for us."

"That's good to hear." Jillian hoped he meant what she thought he did. *He wants to spend his life with me.*

After browsing gift shops and collecting shells most all afternoon, Jillian could hardly wait to be alone with Travis.

"Would you like to go for a moonlit boat ride?" He asked, taking her hand in his as they walked back to his condo.

"No, I think we can find other ways of entertaining ourselves." She'd been on moonlit cruises before with Thomas and knew there'd be other love struck couples. She couldn't do what she had in mind in the company of others.

Back at the condo, they stripped off their sweaty clothes. The sight of his hard naked body took her breath away, causing her to gasp with passion. She could only stare, wanting him with her whole being. When he came up from behind, she melted into his embrace.

This brought back memories and for an instant she felt as if she were in Thomas's arms again. He had the same strong shoulders and the same soft lips. Feeling dizzy for a moment, she almost thought it was Thomas. *How foolish, Thomas is dead.* Was it possible God sent her someone so much like Thomas to take his place?

****

"Are you sure you want me to take you home?" Travis asked the following morning. "We can stay here tonight and I'll drive you to work tomorrow."

"I'd love to, but I have so much to do before our Paris trip."

"Does that mean you've decided to go?"

"Yes. Now take me home so I can get things done."

When Jillian arrived home, Suzette's car sat parked in the drive way.

"What are you doing home so early? I expected you to stay the night and go to school with Tara as you usually do." Jillian made herself a cup of tea and sat down at the table across from Suzette.

"I'm not feeling well. Maybe I'm coming down with something." Suzette held her head back as Jillian felt for a fever.

"You don't feel warm. Maybe you should go lie down."

"I think I will. Good Night Mom. I love you."

"Good Night Dear, I love you too."

Jillian's cell rang Monday morning on her way to the office. 'Melody Mendoza' showed up on the display.

"Hi Mel, what's up."

"I'm sorry, but I have to cancel getting together again. I'm going to Alaska to do a decorating job. For security reasons, I can't tell you who it's for."

"I can imagine. Does she wear glasses and have dark brown hair?"

"You guessed it!" Jillian laughed. "Now what's new with you?"

"I feel like hell this morning after tossing and turning all night long. I had the weirdest dreams of Thomas, or maybe Travis. I don't know who, maybe both in one. The man in my dreams talked and felt like Thomas, but I called him Travis and he called me "Teddy Bear". Thomas never called me that, he always called me by my name."

"Do you know everything about Travis? Have you run a background check on him?"

"Why should I do that?"

"In this day and time, it's the wise thing to do. You'd be surprised how many men are out to con women. And you fit the profile of some of those women."

Chapter Four

"I hope our plane is on time," Jillian said as they arrived at JFK.

"We should arrive at Charles de Gaulle in seven hours. Of course it'll be midnight there."

"There'll be a full moon tonight, a good time to see the sights from our hotel window." Jillian's pulse raced at the thought of being in the city of light with the man she loved.

"We'll be staying at the George V. The Le Cinq Restaurant there has the best food in France."

Arriving at the hotel, Jillian wanted to do something romantic.

"Would you like to sit on the terrace?"

"After the flight I just want to relax, have a glass of champagne, and be with the woman I love." He kicked off his shoes, sitting on the lush leather sofa.

"That sounds romantic enough for me." She poured the champagne, sat down beside him, and snuggled closer. Unbuttoning his shirt, she trailed kisses up and down his chest, trying to arouse him.

"Not tonight Teddy Bear. The flight was long and tiring and the baby crying across the aisle made it seem even longer. Maybe tomorrow night we'll take a gondola ride."

She didn't let her disappointment show, but sat quietly watching a movie until Travis fell asleep on the sofa. Jillian didn't have the heart to wake him, instead, she took a shower and went to bed alone.

The morning sun shone through the blinds, lighting up the room. Jillian rose on one elbow to discover Travis already gone. *He must be in the lobby getting breakfast.* When in an hour he didn't return, she got up, dressed, and called room service.

"I'd like two eggs, scrambled with a wheat croissant."

Two hours later Travis returned, bringing chocolates and flowers.

"Hey Teddy Bear get dressed and we'll go for breakfast." He put his arms around her, nuzzling her neck.

"I ordered eggs and croissants. If I'd known when you'd return I'd have ordered for you, but I had no idea." Jillian chose her words carefully, so as not to sound accusing.

"I couldn't sleep and didn't want to wake you, so I went for a walk," he said.

"That's fine, let me order you some breakfast." It hurt her that he'd gone out without her, but she couldn't let it ruin her trip.

"I'll grab something later." He took off his shoes and lay down on the sofa.

"I think we should go out and see the sights. Are you up to it?" She lay down beside him.

"I'm sorry Teddy Bear, I must be getting old. The walk tired me out. Why don't you go out and see the sights. After a short nap, we'll do something."

Again, disappointment filled her, but after all, they still had the whole week ahead of them. Maybe it'd turn into two weeks, depending on how long it took him to finish his business. There'd be plenty of time to see the sights.

Looking out over the beautiful view from the terrace, she wished Travis would reconsider and go with her, but he'd already begun snoring. She wasn't into going out in a strange place by herself, yet she didn't want to sit in the hotel room while Travis slept. She could come back in two hours, which would give him a good long nap. She might even go back to bed with him, and they'd probably end up making love before going out for lunch. Afterwards they'd have a wonderful evening taking in the sights.

She'd been to Paris once before. While married to Thomas, they'd come here on a business trip, which turned out to be a wonderful vacation. They spent days seeing the sights and nights making love. They'd planned on coming back, but never got the chance. Tears filled her eyes.

Getting out of the elevator, she walked through the lobby with its beautiful tapestries covered furniture and bronze sculptures. Jillian felt lost in such a big place. She thought about going back upstairs to the safety of Travis' arms, but there were so many things here to see. She felt drawn onto the street and into the crowds of tourist with their cameras and zest for excitement. The smell of sausages and sweets filled the air, making her wish she hadn't eaten.

Walking by a shop which rented bicycles, she decided it'd be fun to ride. She reached into her purse, taking out the Euros needed for the rental. She hadn't ridden a bike since age fifteen. *Can I still ride one?* Getting on the bike, she recalled the old saying 'just like riding a bike'. Putting her feet on the petals, it came back to her as if she'd been riding all these years.

Riding along streets with names she couldn't pronounce, she wished she'd brought her camera. Feelings of excitement built inside her as she watched lovers holding hands and kissing. She fantasized about Travis and imagined him by her side, holding her hand as they strolled along the canal. Caught up in the fantasy, she didn't realize she'd whispered words of love aloud. It embarrassed her when a young American man stopped in front of her.

"Are you alright Miss?"

"I'm fine, just reciting a poem I used to know," she lied.

Before she knew it, she'd ridden for over two hours and had no idea which way to get back. She'd crossed over from one side of the street to the other so many times she'd confused herself. *I'll have to ask directions.*

Luckily, she could speak some French. She'd taken a semester in high school and knew that 'S'il Vous' means Please and 'Merci' means thank you. Maybe she could get directions from an American. Seems there were so many more American tourists in Paris than any other nationality.

Riding past a monument, she noticed a man with a camera photographing a woman and two children. As she came closer she could hear them talking. They were American.

"Come on Daddy, can we go for a ride on the boat?" one of the children said pleadingly.

"Excuse me sir. Could you give me some directions?" Telling him where she needed to go, it relieved her to find they were staying nearby.

"Yes I know the way there. Take a right at the light, go three blocks then another right at the stop sign."

"Thank you. Enjoy your visit here."

Arriving back at the hotel, she got into the elevator and hurried up to the room, ignoring the bellman standing by to assist her. She couldn't wait to share the details of her adventures with Travis. She could imagine his smile when she told him about renting a bike for touring the city.

Running into the bedroom of the suite, she expected Travis to be waiting for her. The chocolates on the pillows told her the housekeepers had been in to make the beds and freshen up the room. She called his name, but got no answer. Where could he be? Then she saw the note on the table.

Sorry, Teddy Bear.

I forgot I have a meeting today.

See you later. Love Travis

Fury filled her, she knew he'd come to Paris on business, but why did he want her to come? She imagined it'd be different. She remembered going on business trips with Thomas. The summer Suzette turned two they spent three months in the Florida Keys on business. Night after night, they made love under the stars. Sometimes they slept on the Terrace of their suite at the Little Palm Island Resort. Such sweet memories...

Snapping back to reality, she walked out onto the terrace, watching the beautiful people below. Some already dressed for the evening, reminded her of the pink sundress she'd bought at Eva's Fashion Boutique before leaving home. A backless, knee length dress fit her slim waist like a glove and showed off her shapely legs. She'd been going to the gym and working out on her lunch hour and sometimes after work.

Stripping away her sweaty cloths, she got into the shower. The hot water and luxurious shower gel felt like Heaven to her after being out in the sun most of the day. Although cooler here than back home, wearing slacks and a long sleeve shirt, she'd worked up a sweat.

Putting on the pink dress, she took an approving look in the mirror. Luckily, she'd brought a silk jacket to cover her arms. The digital clock read ten after five. She wondered where Travis could be and why he hadn't called. She checked the answering service of the hotel, but no messages.

Finally, at seven o'clock she heard his key in the door, and felt relieved.

"Where have you been? I've missed you terribly," she said.

"I'm so sorry Teddy Bear; the meeting went longer than I anticipated. Are you hungry? Let's go down to the Le' Cing and have dinner. I'm craving the Sea Bass, with some strawberry sorbet for desert," he said teasingly.

She didn't expect him to be so late. Her stomach growled from hunger.

"I'm so hungry I will eat anything." They both laughed as he pulled her close, nuzzling her neck.

They had the lobster tart for the first course, followed by the French bean salad. By the time the final course came, Jillian felt tipsy from the wine. She never drank much, but tonight she couldn't help herself, the music set the perfect ambiance for romance. She could hardly wait to get back to the room.

Her head reeled with love for Travis. *Is tonight the night he'll ask me to marry him?* Alone in the elevator, she nuzzled his neck and nibbled his ear. *Maybe that's where he'd been… out shopping for an engagement ring.*

Travis put the key card into the lock, guiding her inside. She went into the bathroom, took off the dress, feeling disappointed that he didn't even notice it. *I won't let it bother me, not tonight.* She had too much to look forward to. She brushed her hair until it shone, before slipping on the see-thru teddy she'd hung in the bathroom earlier that day. After brushing her teeth, she moisturized her lips with a pink lip gloss, making them look fuller.

Going to the built-in stereo, she put on some soft mood music, and dimmed the lights. She could hear the sound of Travis' soft, even breathing as she walked seductively into the room. Her bubble burst when she heard him snore. *How could he?*

She slipped into bed and tried cuddling with him, but by this time, she knew there was no use. He must have had a busy day. They still had the entire week left to be together.

Next morning she called room service.

"I'd like to order coffee and croissants." They could lie leisurely in bed and talk over their plans for the day.

"That was thoughtful of you Teddy Bear, but I have to take a shower and go to the office." Travis got up, after the shortest love making session on record, leaving her lying in bed. *Why did I even come to Paris?*

"Will you be back soon?" She dreaded another day alone.

"I have meetings all morning, but should be finished by four."

She could be home spending time with Suzette or friends from work. On second thought, she didn't have many friends at work. If truth be known she didn't have any. She made a mental note to get out more.

Hearing Travis' cell phone ring surprised her. *He must have forgotten it.* She tried to ignore it, but it kept beeping. Picking up the phone, she intended to turn it off, but when it started ringing again, she answered it. *It may be Travis calling to see where he left it.*

"Hello." Expecting to hear Travis say, 'Hello Teddy Bear,' as he always did, it shocked her hearing a woman's voice.

"You must be Stephan's secretary. Would you put him on the line please?"

"No Ma'am. You must have the wrong number; there's no one by the name of Stephen here."

"I'm sorry I thought I called Stephen's cell phone."

"No…wrong number."

"I'm sure I dialed the correct number, must be a glitch in the cell tower."

"Yes… must be."

"That's strange…," the woman said before hanging up the phone.

The previous evening repeated itself. They had dinner at the hotel restaurant, ordered the same thing, and afterwards Travis fell asleep while she got ready for bed. *It's as if we're already married.* And he hadn't even popped the question yet.

She'd forgotten all about the phone call that she'd received earlier.

The following few days remained the same. He'd leave in the mornings and after dinner he'd fall asleep before she came to bed. However, the mornings were wonderful. They had a few hours together before he left for his office. She couldn't complain; after all, he came here to sell his business so he could spend more time with her.

Chapter Five

"The doctor released me. I can hardly wait for you to get here," Felicia said.

"I'll be there in a couple hours," Stephan said.

"I'm anxious to get home and start being a wife again. Could you come sooner?"

"I'm working on a business deal Teddy Bear. I'll get there as soon as I can."

Felicia dressed in a white silk pantsuit, thankful Stephen waited for her to come out of the coma. Most men wouldn't wait that long. That proved he loved her, regardless of what her mother said.

She shivered, thinking back to the accident that sent her into a coma. Stephan called around noon that Friday, explaining that he had to work late at the office. He wanted her to meet him for a night out. It being their first year anniversary, he'd given her the car, a pearl white Mercedes. Who'd have thought the brakes would fail on a brand new car?

Fastening her diamond necklace, she heard the light knock on the door. She loved that about him, always punctual. When she woke up three weeks earlier, she'd asked the doctor not to tell Stephan. She wanted to wait until she could walk and talk properly again, to surprise him. She thought he'd have a heart attack the day he came in to find her sitting up in the bed.

"Hey Teddy Bear you look beautiful," he said, bringing her back to the present. He put his arms around her, kissing her on the cheek.

"It's about time you got here. You seem so much busier now than before my accident." She snuggled closer to him, holding him tight. "It's so good to be near you again."

It seemed only yesterday they were happily married, living in a beautiful penthouse apartment in scenic downtown Paris, overlooking the Seine River.

"I got held up with a client, and couldn't get away any sooner. Are you ready to go?" He picked up a small suitcase from the floor.

"Yes, I've been ready since I woke up from the coma, but knew I had to finish my physical therapy." She took him by the arm as they walked out of the hospital room together.

"I'm so excited. Have you done any redecorating in the apartment?"

"I haven't changed a thing. I couldn't bear to."

"You seem a million miles away. What's on your mind?"

"I'm thinking now you're awake, maybe we can go on a vacation as soon as I wrap up this business deal I'm working on."

"What kind of business deal?"

"I'm selling my New York location and will operate only from the Paris office. I have to meet with the gentlemen interested in buying me out."

"Will they be coming here to meet?"

"No. I have to go there, but it won't be for long. When I come back we're going on a vacation."

"Maybe we can go back to Aruba and stay at the Bucuti Beach Resort where we spent our honeymoon." They'd spent endless nights making love on the white sand beaches there. One night getting drunk on Balashi beer from the local brewery, they slept in a chaise lounge by the pool. Smiling at the memory, she knew they'd make many more memories together.

"Yes Teddy Bear, I wanted it to be a surprise. So when I'm working all those hours, don't accuse me of neglecting you. It's so we'll have longer to stay in Aruba. I hope at least a month."

He'd always called her "Teddy Bear", and she loved it, yet sometimes she kidded him about forgetting her name. Marcella, her mother, always said he had other women and didn't want to slip up calling one by the wrong name.

How her mother felt about Stephan was a long…story. She'd accused him of dealing drugs along with other illegal activities.

"He's just like your father. I know he's doing something that's against the law. You'll never know what he does for a living, just like I was with William. You'd best stay away from that one, he's trouble." Her mother would rave on and on.

Felicia's father, a mobster, died the year she turned fifteen, leaving enough money, so she'd never have to work. The only stipulation being, she'd gain control of it when she turned twenty-five. The seven bedroom mansion that William had built for them would also go to Felicia upon her mother's death.

When Felicia turned twenty, she married her college sweetheart, Richard McMinn, while he took leave from the Army. Richard, an only child of famous Hollywood producer Howard McMinn, died nine months later. Taliban Militants attacked his patrol, shooting him to death. Again Felicia inherited a large sum of money and an empty mansion.

She thought she'd never marry again, thinking no one could measure up to her precious Richard. Only a year later she met Stephan. He seemed so much like Richard, even walked and talked like him. Sometimes she almost forgot that he wasn't her late husband. After dating only a few months, he asked her to marry him. Her mother objected, not only because she didn't trust him, but because he was twenty years older than Felicia. Regardless of what her mother said about him, she loved him. Two months later, she slipped away to marry him. Her mother cried like a baby when Felicia told her she was moving three hundred miles away to live in Pariswither new husband. That was their last time together. However, they still talked on the phone once or twice a year.

"It's just like I remember," Felicia said, walking into the apartment after being away for a year. She'd wanted her husband to carry her over the threshold, as he did when they first married, but he complained that his back hurt.

Everything was still in place as she'd left it. Even the lounging gown she'd taken off the night of her accident still lay across the foot of the bed. She'd thrown it down there when she changed into her evening clothes. She smiled, remembering the beautiful dress she wore that night.

"I'd like to take a shower before dinner." Stephan headed down the hall toward the bathroom. "I wish now I'd called the cleaning lady in. Dust is everywhere."

"Are we going out to dinner or do you want to order in?" Felicia asked, beginning to get hungry. Since awakening over three weeks earlier, she'd only had hospital food. The doctors run so many tests, her recovery amazed them. They called it a miracle that she'd come out of it unharmed, with no brain damage.

"I thought we'd stay in tonight and get some rest. We need to make sure you're all well before we start going out. I don't want you to exhaust yourself; after all you have been asleep for a year."

"That's right! A year I've been resting, now I'm ready to see the world on my handsome husband's arm."

"There's plenty of time for that after you're stronger." He shut the bathroom door.

Ordering from Kok Ping, her favorite Chinese restaurant, they had dinner delivered.

After dinner, they watched the stock market report.

"I'm going to bed." Felicia said, yawning. "I don't know why I'm so tired."

****

Stephan had slipped two of the sleeping pills, prescribed by Felicia's doctor, into her glass of red wine. She'd be out at least eight hours or longer, which would give him time to get to Jillian.

He put on fresh cologne before leaving the apartment. He'd explain to her that he'd fallen asleep at the office and hoped she wouldn't be mad at him.

Arriving in the cab, he looked up to see her sitting on the terrace, looking beautiful in the moonlight. He imagined holding her, whispering endearments in her ear while they made love on the terrace, as they'd done one night since being in Paris.

Unlocking the door, he stepped inside. She had every right to be upset. Checking his cell phone earlier, he saw that she'd tried calling him several times. He'd turned the ringer off. Walking through the hotel suite and out onto the terrace, he slipped his arms around her.

"Hey there Teddy Bear, I knew you were out here, I saw you from the street." He nuzzled her neck, knowing that's what she liked.

Jumping up, she threw her arms around his neck.

"I thought you'd been in an accident," she said, trembling. He'd forgotten about her ex-husband dying in an automobile crash, of course she'd think that way.

"I'm fine...I fell asleep at the office, that's all."

"I saved dinner for you. When you weren't here by eight, I ordered room service and there is plenty leftover."

"I grabbed a sandwich on the way," he lied.

Next morning he slipped up at daybreak, hung a note on the refrigerator, and left. He had to plan his next move. *What will I do about Felicia?* He'd have to come up with something. He used to be attracted to her, but now realized that money attracted him. When they married, he didn't know her father had tied her money up in a trust fund. She had no access to it until her twenty-fifth birthday, two more years. Now he wanted Jillian, her husband died, leaving her millions. He'd read about his death in the newspapers. Thomas Bradford, a very wealthy man, made his millions in advertising.

22

Chapter Six

Dear Teddy Bear I had an early appointment.

See you tonight.   Love You, Travis

Taking the note off the fridge, she threw it in the trash. *I wish I'd never come to Paris.* She hardly got to see Travis at all. When she did, he complained of being tired from working all day. He couldn't even take her out to see the sights. The first week she'd shopped, picking up souvenirs for friends and clothes and accessories for Suzette. She knew how her daughter loved dressing in the latest fashions. She took that after her father, he'd always dressed for success.

Another disappointment, she sat down on the sofa, turning on the television. Watching Regis and Kelly gave her an idea.

I'll call Travis and ask him if he wants company for lunch. She could meet him at a restaurant near his office. She picked up the phone and dialed his cell number.

"Hello," a female voice said.

Why is a woman answering Travis' cell phone? She started to hang up, but instead regained her composure.

"Could I speak to Travis please?" Her voice trembled.

"You must have the wrong number, there's no one by that name here."

Jillian slammed down the phone, recognizing the voice as the woman who'd called for Stephan a few days earlier. How could she ever forget that whiny voice? She'd never heard such a mixture of broken English and French. She must be one of Travis's associates or maybe his secretary. *Maybe he's having an affair with her. No...he couldn't be.* She pushed the thought out of her mind.

Turning back to the TV, she watched as Ellen Degeneres announced the guests for the day. Charlie Sheen's face flashed across the screen along with the winner of American Idol. She'd heard of the show, but never watched it. People watch too much TV and don't spend enough time with their families was her take on the subject. She'd much rather do things with Suzette than sit in front of a TV.

After twenty to thirty minutes of annoying television shows, Jillian picked up the remote pushing the power button off. She'd never been one to sit still for long at a time. She had to be doing something. More shopping might relieve the boredom. Maybe she'd find some early Christmas gifts. She let out a sigh. *What a wasted trip.*

Seems she'd been in every shop in town at least twice and it didn't take long before being bored to tears. Walking past the movie theatre, she looked at the marquee. *That's a good way to spend the afternoon.* There again, she found the movie of little interest and left the theatre during intermission.

Ducking into a flower shop, she purchased a bouquet of fresh cut flowers. *Maybe they'll brighten up the hotel room somewhat.* This trip had turned out to be a disappointment, but at least she'd bought lots of gifts for Suzette and friends back home.

With only a few days left in Paris, Jillian wanted desperately for Travis to go sightseeing with her. She didn't want the trip to be a total loss. She purchased an irresistible new outfit, planning to wear it for him that evening. *How could he say no to me dressed in this?*

The leather slacks fit her snugly and the halter top showed off the spray tan she'd gotten earlier that week. After brushing her hair until it shown, she put on a pair of gold hoop earrings and a hint of mascara. She didn't look her age at all. Most people, who knew her, said she looked to be in her early thirties instead of forties. She put on a coating of pale pink lip-gloss and pressed her lips together before looking into the mirror. She smiled approvingly.

Hearing Travis's key in the door, Jillian rushed to welcome him.

"There's my Teddy Bear!" Travis walked straight into her arms.

"I can't believe you're actually here this early. And to what do I owe this pleasure?" She took his jacket and loosened his tie, kissing him passionately.

"I've finished my business here and we're going home."

"What about sightseeing? There's so many things I want to share with you."

"I've had enough of Paris for a while. We'll come back soon to take in all the sights. I promise."

"So why don't we go out and celebrate our last night in Paris?" she asked him pleadingly.

"I have a better idea. Why don't we stay in and celebrate our last night here?" He winked, assuring her of what he meant.

"That's fine by me too." *Maybe we'll come back to Paris on our honeymoon.*

They spent the entire evening in bed making up for the last two weeks. He knew exactly how to make her forget her anguish.

Chapter Seven

Felicia, Devastated that Stephan had to go out of town on business so soon after her recovery. She'd hoped he'd stay home with her for at least a few more days, until she got back into the groove of things. *What will I do to stay busy?* She didn't have any friends here in the city. The friends she had back home stopped calling when she married Stephan, because she no longer had time for them. Her new husband took up all her spare time and that's the way she wanted it.

For certain, she planned to have a decorator come in. The place needed updating badly. Seeing Melody Mendoza on TV had given her the idea. She'd heard of the famous interior decorator from New York, who had the reputation of being the best in the world. She looked her up in the yellow pages, planning to give her a call later. First of all, she wanted to go out and see the city. She loved Paris and always enjoyed strolling up and down the streets and browsing in the shops. Maybe she'd get some decorating ideas.

Dressing in jeans, she put her hair in a ponytail, letting it fall to one side. Stephan liked it that way. She missed him already. Thinking of him brought tears to her eyes. He'd proved his love by waiting for her to come out of the coma.

Walking along cobblestone streets, Felicia breathed in the aroma of patisseries and ice cream parlors. Shop windows sparkled with fine china and crystal. She browsed furniture and décor shops, getting ideas for the apartment. start here

Buying a notebook, she took notes on designer pieces she wanted to incorporate into her home. Things had changed so much while she'd been in the coma. It was like being in Paris for the first time. The china restaurant, she loved so much, hadn't changed, but new shops lined both sides of the street.

After filling several pages in the notebook, she walked toward the apartment in case Stephan called. She needed a cell phone, and made herself a mental note to get one the following day. A computer is something she could use also; she used to go to the library anytime she needed to get on line. Stephan never wanted a computer in the house because he said it invaded their privacy, having to give so much personal information.

Her husband called as soon as she walked through the door. She'd barely had time to take off her jacket before the phone rang.

"Hello. Hoffman residence," she said with pride.

"Hello Mrs. Hoffman. How's my Teddy Bear?"

"I'm wonderful now that you've called. When are you coming home?"

"I've only been gone one day, and have tons of business to take care of here. Why don't you go to the ocean for a few days and relax? It'll make the time go faster."

They had a beautiful oceanfront home in Ocean City, Maryland. They'd bought it with the money from the sale of her house. Stephan advised her it'd be a good investment. They talked about retiring there someday.

"I wouldn't want to go there without you…besides I have things to do here in the apartment."

"That's fine dear. I just want you to be happy and not over-do it. Remember you just came out of a coma and the doctors don't want you under any stress."

"I'm not under stress; I just got back from a shopping trip. Wait until you get home and hear what I have planned."

"I have to get back to work Teddy Bear. I'll call you tomorrow, it'll be late when I finish tonight and I wouldn't want to disturb you."

Chapter Eight

Jillian sat waiting for Travis when he walked through the door. She wasn't happy about the way things happened in Paris, but she loved and respected him more than ever. While in France, he'd confided in her how he'd started with nothing and built the business to a multimillion-dollar company. Just like Thomas had done with his business. That's one thing that truly impressed her with him, another was the way he dressed in his Brioni suits, and his Berluti shoes. He made her think of her father. From the time she was a little girl, she always knew she wanted to marry a man who wore clothes like her daddy. Travis's taste was identical to his. Her first husband was a good dresser also. She loved a well-dressed man and she'd always taught her daughter how to dress to impress.

She snuggled up to Travis as he settled down on the brown leather sofa. He put his arms around her, pulling her closer. She'd waited for this moment all day and wanted it to be perfect. Last night in the middle of their lovemaking, he told her he loved her more than anything else in the world, and didn't want to live without her. She just knew he'd pop the question tonight. He probably would have last night if the phone hadn't rang just as he poured out his heart. Suzette called to tell her she wouldn't be home over the weekend. She'd planned a camping trip with friends. Travis fell asleep while they talked. She hoped they'd take up tonight where they left off last night.

"You smell delicious," he said as he got a whiff of the Chanel No.5. She'd purchased it in Paris, but hadn't worn it until now. Her friend Melody always wore it and she loved smelling it. She wanted tonight to be special. After getting her hair trimmed and hi-lighted today, she'd gone shopping for a sexy sheer negligee. She'd make sure he'd never forget tonight.

Jillian put a bottle of Don Perignon White Gold on ice to serve in Vera Wang toasting flutes, a wedding gift from Thomas' parents. She'd packed them away after her husband's death because looking at them only brought back his memory. He'd always enjoyed using them, whether they had company or just the two of them. Someday they'd belong to Suzette as heirlooms from her grandparents.

"Let's make a toast," she said, getting up to pour the champagne into the flutes. Travis's eyes took notice of the expensive glasses. She felt pride in his good taste.

"I'll have to say, you know how to spoil a guy." He took the glass she handed him.

"Hold on for just a moment, until I slip into something more comfortable." She rushed for the stairs and then toward her bedroom. A few moments later, she returned.

"Who were you talking to?" she asked as he put his cell phone back into his pocket. "Whoever it is…tell them you have something more important to attend to."

She walked slowly toward him in nothing but a pair of stilettos and bright red lipstick. She'd decided not to put on the negligee. Why waste the time? He'd take it right back off. She'd worn dozens of sexy outfits for him, but she'd never initiated their lovemaking in this way. Usually she stayed reserved and modest, but tonight she had a mission.

"Oh, it was nobody…just a client. I told him I'd call him back later, maybe I'll call him after dinner…and then maybe I won't." He pulled her down on his lap, kissing her long and hard. "I love you so much."

"I love you too." She removed his tie and unbuttoned his shirt. Before long they'd forgotten about everything, but each other.

After an hour or longer, Travis sat up, picked up his glass, and toasted.

"To us… hoping we stay together for a long time."

"I'll drink to that." She tipped her glass against his. She wanted to be with him for a long time, hopefully for the rest of her life. She knew he loved her; but didn't know if he wanted to marry her…maybe he just needed a little push.

She got up, motioning him to follow her. He did…straight to the bedroom, forgetting all about dinner.

****

The weekend ended much too soon and with Suzette coming home on Sunday, Travis would have to go back to his own house. He didn't ask her to marry him, even with the little pushes she'd given him. Once she'd almost come out and asked him. It was earlier that morning and they'd just finished a breakfast of waffles with strawberry topping. He loaded the dishwasher while she put the sheets from her bed in the washer. After making love on them more than ten times, they'd need a little extra wash time. She set the washer on extra heavy load and came back to the kitchen.

"This is what marriage is going to feel like," she said as she patted him on the butt and poured herself a second cup of coffee. She expected him to come back with a confirmatory answer, but he didn't.

"What cycle should I set the dishwasher on?"

She felt like giving up. From now on she'd let him take the initiative. He'd pop the question eventually, she felt sure of it. He already spent all his spare time with her.

Travis had been gone only an hour when Suzette came home.

"I'm starved Mom, are you going to fix breakfast soon?"

Jillian didn't want Suzette to know that her lover spent the night, actually the weekend.

"Yes dear. I'm glad you're home. Did you have a good time?" She took pancake flour out of the pantry.

"Yes Mother, I had a wonderful time, and I have a surprise for you."

"What is it?"

"I'll wait until after breakfast to tell you. Right now I'm going to take a hot shower." Suzette headed for the stairs.

Jillian thought of Travis as she took the dishes from the dishwasher. He'd done a lousy job of loading them, but at least they came clean. She could have left them for Sonya, the housekeeper, but somehow it made her feel close to him. The thoughts of the last two nights made her smile. They'd made love so many times, yet she still desired him. She could never get enough of him.

Coming back into the kitchen thirty minutes later, Suzette wore a clean shorts outfit.

"Aren't you going to eat Mom?" She took a big bite of the pancakes and sausage.

"No dear, I had breakfast earlier."

"You mean you ate alone? Knowing I'd be home soon." Suzette teased her.

"I woke up hungry because I didn't have dinner last night."

"Oooooh…and what were you doing that you'd miss dinner for?" Suzette continued to tease her.

"Stop it! I cleaned my closet, taking out some clothes that have been there for years. By the way, we need to go shopping. I would love to buy one of those cute little sundresses with no straps. I also need new make-up. Do you want to go tomorrow?"

"Tomorrow is not good for me. I have a job interview." Suzette took her last bite and put the plate into the sink.

"And what company is the interview with?"

"Riggs & Straus advertising," Suzette threw caution to the wind, telling her mother everything about the job offer. I want to follow my father's example.

"But that's all the way inside the city, too far for your to drive every day." She'd always thought her daughter would go to work for Bradford's Advertising, part-time until she graduated college, then take a full-time position.

"Yes it'd be too far to drive every day. If I accept the job, I'll move into an apartment there."

This made Jillian nervous, her daughter just turned eighteen. She'd never been that far away from home, except to go on spring break with friends, and then she didn't even stay the night. She took the next flight back home after having an argument with one of the other girls. The only comforting factor in the situation was that her best friend, Melody Mendoza, lived in the city and could probably check in on Suzette occasionally, if she decided to take the job there.

The offer Riggs & Straus advertising firm made Suzette was one she couldn't refuse. They offered her a generous salary and even offered to cover her relocation cost. The only stipulation was that she'd continue with her education in the advertising field. Knowing the history of her late father, they said she'd be an asset to their company. Mr. Riggs had at one time made him a good offer, but he turned them down for a better offer. He didn't want this to happen with Thomas Bradford's daughter.

Jillian accompanied her daughter to New York for the job interview. They'd gone on-line, searching for apartments and found five in areas that'd be safe for a young woman to live. After looking all day they narrowed it down to only three. Each had benefits and it excited Suzette to be on her own, but again, left her apprehensive about leaving her mother.

"You can come to New York and spent the weekend sometime and we'll go shopping or to a play," she told Jillian.

"That'd be fun." Jillian didn't like the idea of her daughter being in the city alone, yet realized it'd be easier for her to be alone with Travis now. He could stay overnight more often, and he'd see that marriage to her would be perfect.

Suzette decided on a two-bedroom walk-up on the fifth floor in East Village, having a spectacular view of Second Avenue. She loved the spacious closets, and she'd have a second bedroom for when her mother came to spend the weekends.

The fashion boutiques and the many ethnic restaurants lined both sides of the street. Suzette couldn't wait to try some of the food and go shopping in the stores.

"Why don't we hire Melody to decorate for you?" Jillian asked Suzette when they went to sign the lease for the apartment.

"No Mom. I want to do it all myself."

"But when will you have the time dear? What, with your new job and your studies."

"I can check out furniture and linens on-line, but it'd be so much more fun to browsing the boutiques and art galleries here."

"Well if you change your mind let me know and I'll give Melody a call. It'd be a great chance for the two of you to spend time together."

Chapter Nine

Suzette loved her new job. Everyone at Riggs & Riggs treated her with respect. She knew her father's reputation had something to do with it. Not only here, but big advertising firms all over the country had made him offers to come to work for them. She only hoped she could live up to that reputation.

Her small office didn't have a beautiful view of the city as she'd have liked, but she didn't care. She'd work her way up to a beautiful corner office with a gorgeous view before long. She had faith in herself, a chip off of the old block. Her father had been the best in the business. She couldn't mess up because of the high bar he'd set. Thinking of the father that she barely remembered brought tears to her eyes. *Wouldn't it be wonderful if he were here to see me now, dressed in my silk-twill del pelato shift dress and Manolo Blahnik leather pumps.* Her mother had always taught her to dress nicely and she didn't cut corners when it came to making a good impression. Of course, thanks to her father, she'd never had to cut corners at all.

If only her father had lived, things would have been different, yet she couldn't have had a better life. When he died, her mother took her to her grandparents, where she stayed for several weeks. She loved staying with Nana and Papa. She'd have stayed there all the time if her mother let her. The big rambling old house they lived in reminded her of a castle with surprises in every room. She spent hours looking at photo albums or watching films of her mother as a child. Sometimes they'd go fishing, and she always caught the most fish, of course as she got older she realized that Papa put the fish on her line. She loved her grandparents as much as she loved her parents and she'd always cried when she had to leave them.

For several years after her father's death, she would spend the summers with Nana and Papa. Looking back now, she knew that's what helped her get through it. When her grandparents died, she grieved for months, not only for their death, but because there was no way her mother could help her, she was grieving too.

Just reminiscing about her father and grandparents broke Suzette's heart. Not because they were bad memories, she had only wonderful memories of them. Having this new job and a new apartment made her think of them more often. If only they were here for her to share her joy with.

Suzette loved coming home to her very own place. Sometimes one of the girls from work would stop by for coffee and they'd share a cab to the office. Looking through magazines she'd gotten many ideas on how to decorate, she'd already purchased a CR-Perla sectional sofa and a huge plasma TV for the living room. She still needed bedroom furniture, but hadn't found exactly what she wanted yet. Like her mother, she wanted something she could keep for a long time and not grow tired of. Her mother still had the same furniture she'd bought before her father died. She had it cleaned once a year and moved it around to give the room a different look. Sometimes she'd buy different drapes or throw rugs, but when Suzette tried to get her to buy new furniture she'd tell her how much she loved her Italian suede sofa and chairs.

The pale beige walls of the apartment reminded Suzette of the beaches in Florida. She would sometimes lie down on the floor to watch TV and pretend to be on the beach in Miami, her favorite place to go. She'd gone there with her mother almost every year as a child. Thinking of their vacations there gave her the idea to have murals of palm trees and the ocean painted on her walls. Looking through the yellow pages, she found the phone number of an artist who came highly recommended by one of the guys from work. He'd hired him to paint a train station on his bedroom wall. He'd grown up in New Mexico near the railroad tracks and wanted to have a memory of it.

The man took two weeks to paint the murals on the living room walls and charged Suzette three thousand dollars. She knew it was expensive, but he'd done it all by hand. She loved it and a week later decided to have a beach scene painted on her bedroom wall. By the time he finished it, she'd gotten to know him pretty well. Raoul Michelot, twenty-four years old, came to New York from France to study Art at NYC. He'd been discovered after painting a mural of Italy's Dolce Aqua on his dorm wall.

The night he finished the bedroom painting, Raoul asked Suzette out to dinner and she accepted. He took her to Gasparino's, a small, but romantic Italian restaurant where they ate Veal Marcella and drank red wine. She enjoyed his company; it was the first time she'd been on an adult date. Back home she'd gone out with guys from high school, to a ball game, the movies, and a few times roller skating. Now she felt so grown up.

After dinner they went for a stroll along the brightly-lit streets. Crowds of young and old alike went in and out of the eateries and fashion boutiques there. This was definitely a place for the adventurous, and she fit right in. She loved it.

Walking along the crowded streets as the evening turned into night, he took her hand in his, pulling her close to him. She didn't resist, feeling as if in a dream. Raoul, the most handsome man she'd ever met, was much more romantic than her high school dates. She let him pull her close as they walked over the small bridge that led to the park. There they found an empty bench and he took her into his arms, kissing her as she'd never been kissed before.

She didn't know if the wine or his kisses made her light-headed, but she found herself not wanting him to stop kissing her. Arriving home at midnight, she wanted to invite him in, but having to get up early, she resisted. That night Suzette dreamed of Raoul and his kisses. She could see his deep-set blue eyes looking into hers. She felt his soft black hair between her fingers. Disappointment filled her when she awoke to find him not there.

Looking at the clock, she realized she'd overslept and had to be at work in half an hour. She jumped up and headed for the shower, putting her hair up in a clip as she went. She wouldn't have time to do anything else with it. Thank God he blessed her with beautiful hair; she got it from her mother. She'd apply her make-up in the cab, on her way to work. She never drove her own car, not wanting to fight the traffic.

From her appearance, one would never know she'd rushed to get ready in fifteen minutes. She had natural beauty, and class to match.

"Good Morning Miss Bradford," Beda, the receptionist said as Suzette entered the front office. Smiling at the girl, she headed down the hallway. As she turned the corner going toward the small room that she used for an office, she noticed a note on the door.

Oh no, they've moved me to the secretarial pool. Walking closer, she reached up and pulled the note down.

Suzette we've moved you to suite 103 on the east side.

Come to my office for the key, your things are already there.

> *Jim*

Oh my! She couldn't contain herself, knowing suite103 was a corner office. There were others waiting in line for it. Of course she'd already nabbed the Shultz Furniture account and the Barclay's Cadillac account in the short time she'd been there, more than the other rookies combined had done.

She walked into Jim's office for the key, "How did I rate a corner office overlooking the park?" she asked her supervisor.

"We got a call from Melody Mendoza, the famous interior designer. She's placed her account with you. You're on a roll girl. Welcome to the family!" He stood, offering his hand to Suzette.

"Thanks."

Walking together to suite 103, he guided her into the beautifully decorated office.

"I love it!" she said in awe. She didn't mention the fact that Melody was her mother's best friend, and she knew her mother hadn't wasted any time making a phone call.

"Let's go to lunch to celebrate, be ready at noon," he said and walked out before she could answer. She didn't know if she was ready for all of this, but knowing she had the 'Bradford' name behind her gave her confidence.

Sitting down at her new desk, she took out her cell phone. She had to call her mother. Maybe she could talk her into coming to New York City soon to spend the weekend. She'd love to show off her new paintings.

Jillian answered the phone after only two rings as if expecting Suzette to call. Melody probably told her she'd given her the account.

"That's wonderful Honey. I'm so happy for you, and yes I'd love to visit the city, it'll give me something to do. With Travis traveling so much now, I hardly see him. I'll call you in a few days and tell you when I can come."

"That's great Mom, see you soon. I love you." She missed her mother and looked forward to spending time with her.

She didn't know yet how she'd tell Raoul of her mother's visit. He'd have to stay at his own apartment. For the last week he'd been staying with her to get the paintings finished. He didn't own a car and she couldn't bear the thought of him taking a cab every day. She wasn't ready to introduce him to Jillian yet. She'd rather wait to see if her relationship with Raoul worked out.

Chapter Ten

"What a wonderful surprise," Felicia said, not expecting Stephan back home so soon after leaving.

"I've missed you, but I can't stay long. I'm working on something really big and I have to be back in New York tomorrow," he said.

"You're kidding…right?" She didn't understand why he'd come back if he had to leave again.

"No. I'm not kidding. I'm sorry. I wish I could stay here in Paris, but I've got work to do."

"Why do you work so much? It's not as if we need the money. We're rich."

"No…You're rich. I make a living by investing other people's money."

"I've often wondered what exactly it is that you do, you're so secretive about your work. I sometimes wonder if your job is legal," she said jokingly.

"Why would you say a thing like that?" He sounded upset.

"I'm only joking. Don't get so defensive." Snuggling up to him, she kissed him on the cheek, remembering how touchy he got when it came to his profession. She recalled one night they'd gone out to dinner with friends and when someone asked Stephan about his work, he clammed up, saying he didn't want to talk shop while out for an enjoyable evening. They'd never gone out again with anyone. Another time she'd asked him about it and he told her it was too complicated to explain. She thought it strange that she knew nothing about his work, but was so much in love with him she didn't question him. Not caring what he did, just as long as he came home to her at night. She was accustomed to her father and the illegal ways he'd made his money, but he'd always given his family the best. She learned as a young girl, not to question it. As she got older she heard people talk and knew that her father's business was something she didn't want to know about. Regardless of his illegal dealings, Felicia loved and admired him.

Being an only child and having the lonely childhood she'd had, Felicia was overwhelmed with happiness now. Knowing she had a loving husband, who waited a year not knowing if she'd come out of her coma, made her the happiest woman alive. Not to mention a husband who loved her so much that he'd interrupted his business trip to come home to her. She was the most fortunate woman in the world.

"I brought your favorite wine. I thought we could have a relaxing night at home and make up for the time that I've had to spend away from you." He pulled a bottle of Domaine Pierre Andre out of his briefcase.

She smiled, knowing what he had in mind.

"Let me put on something more comfortable," she said, heading for the stairs. She didn't expect him for another week and hadn't even put on make-up that morning. Luckily, she'd shaved her legs and shampooed her hair the night before. Hurrying into the bathroom, she took her compact out of the vanity drawer. Having pretty skin, she didn't need a lot of foundation, unlike most red-heads. Just a light dusting of powder and some lipstick would do. Putting on a see-through white negligee, she hoped he like it. She'd ordered it on line and just received it the day before. She'd bought it for her husband's homecoming; thank goodness it arrived early.

She never doubted his love for her and didn't worry that he'd ever cheat on her. He'd told her many times before her accident that she was the only woman for him. She knew he still felt that same way. He'd proved it to her by coming home to see her before his work was finished in New York. He couldn't bear to be away from her, he'd told her that hundreds of times. While Felicia changed cloths and got ready to relax with him, he poured the wine into large wine glasses.

Walking toward him, she smiled, reached out her hand, and took the glass of wine he offered.

"This is good wine," she said after taking a sip.

"Only the best is good enough for my Teddy Bear." He put his arm around her and guided her toward the sofa.

Talking as they drank their wine, Felicia told him how she planned to decorate, but failed to tell him she expected Melody to come anytime.

"What are we going to eat?" She knew the cook wouldn't be in. Stephan arranged her schedule before going to New York.

"How could I think of food when I have you in my arms?"

"Are you trying to get me drunk, so you can take advantage of me?" she joked. Her speech slurred from the wine.

As Felicia lay back onto the sofa, closing her eyes, she dropped the wine glass, spilling wine all over herself and the sofa. The glass shattered into dozens of tiny slivers as it hit the floor.

Chapter Eleven

Reaching into his pocket for the bottle of pills, he took the lid off and poured the remaining pills onto the coffee table. Placing the empty wine bottle in her hands, he wiped up any remaining fingerprints. Now he had to get back to the airport and fly to Connecticut. When he left Jillian the day before, he said he had business in Connecticut. He'd gone there first and checked into a room under the name of Stephan Hoffman. If Jillian called, she'd dial his cell phone.

"Hello Teddy Bear!" he said into the phone as he put the fake passport and credit card far back under the liner in his briefcase.

"How are things in Connecticut? When will you be home?" Jillian asked, happy he'd called. She missed him when he went away on business trips, yet she enjoyed her time with Suzette.

"I'll see you in few days. I love you."

Slipping up the back stairwell to his hotel room, he hoped no one recognized him with the disguise he wore. With the National Business Men's convention going on in town, they'd think he came with them. Several others staggered up the stairs, coming from the lounge. A tall black man, just ahead of him, hung on to some bleached blond he'd picked up, probably a hooker. Anyone could see she wasn't of his class and probably after the gold chain around his neck and the Rolex he wore.

Needing rest before flying home the next evening, he fell onto the bed, feeling a weight lifted from his shoulders. He could sleep like a baby now…or so he thought. Sleep didn't come easy. He had terrible nightmares that kept waking him up. In the first dream, Felicia had switched the glasses of wine and given him the one with the pills in it. He awoke drenched in sweat. In another he dreamed that the police found her and came looking for him. He tried to act upset, but they tricked him into confessing. Just as they opened the prison doors for him to enter, he woke up, again in a sweat.

Fortunately, he'd never associated his name with hers. Only two people knew of their marriage; Marcella, Felicia's mother and Annie, Felicia's elderly grandmother. They lived together in a small town three hundred miles from Paris. He doubted they'd find out for a long time. Probably, when Felicia's grandmother dies, Marcella might try to reach her. He didn't worry, he had an alibi. He'd made a fake call to the front desk from his cell phone, asking for a wake-up call. The half-wit desk clerk would vouch for him.

He didn't know what he'd do until time to go home, it'd look suspicious if he left Connecticut now. He needed to stay at least a few more hours, just for having the sake of an alibi in case the time come when he'd need it.

Opening the door to get the paper, he noticed several men, dressed in suits, standing in the hallway talking. They were there for the convention. That gave him an idea. He'd go down and mingle, meet some people, maybe get some information on how to make his next move. It'd at least give him something to do while pretending to be here on business. He might even meet some people that'd be helpful to him.

He showered and dressed in his black Fioravati business suit, he'd purchased it on one of his 'business trips' to Napoli. Smiling, he thought of the woman he'd gone there to meet. Her husband had been killed a year earlier in a plane crash and she was lonely. He knew just how to wine and dine her at her favorite restaurant, 'Rosiellos'. Before long, he moved into her 2 million dollar mansion and six months later, she invested 10 million dollars with him. He could have stayed around for more, but didn't want to take chances. It was a shame how she died when her brakes failed causing her to go down an embankment into a tree. He immediately changed his identity and hi-tailed it back to the states.

Chapter Twelve

Arriving later than she anticipated, Melody rushed to Felicia's apartment. Felicia Hoffman called her a week ago and asked her to come to Paris and redecorate her apartment there. She'd told Melody that her husband would be out of town and invited her to stay at her home for a few days. She sounded excited about having another female around to talk to. Melody gathered enough information to know how lonely she felt with her husband out of town. She'd worked for this kind before. Money was no object. They'd dream up things to be done, just so they'd have the company of another human.

Ringing the doorbell, she got no answer. She rang it again. *What is that sound coming from inside?* It sounded like someone vomiting. She tried the door handle… unlocked. *Should I go inside?* After all, Felicia assured her it'd be fine for her to stay at her apartment. *That's probably why the door is unlocked…so I can get in.* Melody assumed Felicia would give her a key the following day.

"Hello…Felicia…are you home?" She listened for an answer, but heard nothing. Moving slowly through the apartment, she couldn't imagine the place being any more beautiful. It reminded her of showrooms in furniture galleries she'd shopped in for her rich clients.

There's that sound again. It seemed to be coming from the living room.

Passing through the long luxurious hallway, Melody wished she had knocked louder instead of walking in. She continued slowly until she could see all the way through the huge room. The view of the Seine River from the large bay window almost took her breath away.

"What the hell…?" Melody said in shock, seeing someone lying on the floor face down in her own vomit. Running to her, she picked up her wrist, feeling for a pulse. *She's still alive.* Taking out her cell phone, not wanting to leave the sick girl long enough to find the house phone, she dialed 911. She feared moving her, but managed to pull her face out of the vomit allowing her to breathe easier. That's when she saw the pills on the table and the empty wine bottle lying on the floor. Broken glass covered the white carpet near the sofa and a piece stuck into the woman's cheek, causing blood to stream onto the carpet. This couldn't be Felicia, she seemed so happy over the phone when she told Melody about waking up from a coma. *Why would she now want to take her own life?*

Melody stayed on the line with 911 until she knew the paramedics were on the way. The operator seemed to think she should have more information for them, but she'd told them everything she knew about the situation. In the meantime, she tried to comfort the girl lying on the floor.

"If you can hear me…just hold on a few minutes longer. Help is on the way." She wrung her hands, wishing the paramedics would hurry and arrive. Melody, beside herself, trembled uncontrollably by the time the emergency crew finally arrived at the Hoffman residence.

Carrying a stretcher, a team of paramedics rushed past Melody, one, a tall man, probably in his thirties, the other shorter and fortyish. Putting a breathing apparatus on her face, the medical team worked for several minutes on the woman. When they got her on the stretcher and started out the door, two police officers arrived, one female, probably in her late twenties.

"Hi I'm Sergeant Hopper, what happened here? The female cop looked into Melody's eyes as if she expected her to lie.

She didn't seem at all upset by the scene in the living room. Probably just another day's work for them, yet Melody would probably have nightmares for weeks…maybe months.

"I don't know. I arrived here ten minutes ago and found her lying there. I turned her face so she could breathe but that's all I touched."

The two men loaded Felicia into an ambulance, while the female cop seemed more interested in questioning Melody. Once they had her inside, the older paramedic turned to Melody.

"Are you a relative?"

"No. She's a client. I came to help Mrs. Hoffman redecorate her apartment. The door was unlocked…so I came in. She'd invited me a week ago. This was to be our first meeting."

The police searched the apartment. She told them everything she knew about Felicia, which wasn't much, just what she'd told her during their phone conversation two days earlier. She didn't know anything about her husband and that seemed to be who they were mainly interested in.

The officers stretched yellow tape across the door of the apartment, marking it as police territory, to keep out trespassers. She'd have to go to the hotel after all, which wasn't a problem. She enjoyed staying at the Park Hyatt. She'd stayed there the last several years and loved the impeccable service they gave. She didn't have a reservation, but knew they always had a room for her.

Melody turned, walking away, when one of the cops called to her.

"Ma'am, you'll have to come with us." Good thing the officers could speak fluent English, because she never learned enough French to carry on a decent conversation. They wanted her to come to the station for questioning.

"Can I drop my bags at the hotel?"

"You'll have to do it later." The female cop took her by the arm, leading her to the squad car.

What have I gotten myself into?

After giving her a cup of stale black coffee and asking a few questions, the officer released Melody.

"Don't leave town. We may have other questions for you."

She agreed and called a cab to take her to the hotel. It was after Midnight and she was exhausted. She couldn't wait to sink into the soft feathery bed at the Park Hyatt.

She drifted off as soon as her head hit the pillow. The hours flew by. Seems she'd just gotten into bed when the alarm went off. She'd set it for seven, wanting to get to the hospital early to hear any news on Felicia. She didn't know for sure if it was Felicia in there. The cops hadn't revealed anything they'd found during their search of the apartment. Remembering the picture of a good-looking older man sitting on a table behind the sofa, Melody assumed it was Stephan. He looked like the man Felicia described to her as her husband.

Melody got out of bed, took a shower, and dressed in slacks and a sweater. Brushing her long dark hair back from her face, she put on a light dusting of face powder. She put on lipstick and dabbed Chanel no 5 on her wrists and behind her ears. Hoping Felicia had made it through the night, she headed for the hospital.

Orderlies picked up the breakfast trays as Melody arrived. Looking at the name on the door confirmed that it was, in fact, Felicia Hoffman in the hospital bed.

"Hi, how are you feeling?" Melody asked, walking into the room.

"Not so good, but with the fluid going into my veins…I'm beginning to get my strength back." She gestured to the bags of clear liquid hanging from the pole beside her bed.

"I'm Melody Mendoza." She reached out her hand to Felicia and then on second thought, just patted her arm.

"Nice to meet you Melody, How did you know I was here?"

"I flew in from New York last night. As we planned in our phone conversation, I came to your apartment. You didn't answer the door when I knocked. I heard strange gaggling noises coming from inside, so I walked in, finding you lying face down in your own vomit. I moved your face out of it so you could breathe and called 911."

"Where was my husband?" Felicia looked confused.

"You were alone. Pills were strewn all over the coffee table and broken glass on the floor."

"The last thing I remember is Stephan telling me he planned to sell his business in New York. I must have fallen asleep…and then I remember being sick and trying to get off the sofa."

"Do you remember how many pills you took?"

"I didn't take any pills. I only had a couple glasses of wine. I hadn't eaten anything so the wine must have gone straight to my head and upset my stomach."

Felicia must be delirious thinking her husband was with her. She'd previously told her that he'd be out of town for another week.

"I don't want to tire you. I'll go now so you can rest. Here's the numbers where I can be reached if you need me for anything. Is there anyone you want me to notify?" Melody handed Felicia the piece of notepaper with the phone number of the hotel, her room number, and her cell phone number on it

"Thank you Melody. I don't know anyone else here in the city. The only family I have is my mother and grandmother and they live a distance from here. I doubt very much they'd care."

Melody felt sorry for the young woman. It broke her heart, thinking of her mother not wanting to know what happened to her daughter. She thought of her own daughter, away at college, and how they talked almost daily on the phone.

She couldn't go home until she knew Felicia would be all right. They must have contacted her husband by now. Hopefully he'd arrive soon. It was sad thinking of such a sweet young girl not having anyone to turn to. What would have happened to her if she hadn't found her? At that moment, she felt the full impact of what had occurred. She'd saved Felicia's life. Wow!

Going back to her hotel room, she changed into lounging pajamas, flopped down on the bed, and flicked on the TV. It'd been ages since she'd relaxed like this in the middle of the day. Looking at the clock, she wondered if her husband was up yet. Taking her cell phone out of her purse, she dialed his number.

"Hello...?" he said sleepily.

"Hey Honey...guess what I did last night?"

"You got drunk and danced nude on the table?"

"Something better than that...I saved someone's life!"

"How did that happen?"

"My new client was almost dead when I arrived. I'll tell you all about it when I get home."

"When are you coming home?"

"I just left yesterday. I told you I'd be gone for two weeks. I'll call you later tonight before I go to bed. I love you." She may not stay two weeks, but she'd wait until Felicia got out of the hospital.

Picking up the remote, she flipped through the channels to "All My Children". Erica had really aged, she must be in her fifties or maybe close to sixty now. She remembered cutting class while in college to watch the soaps. They'd crowd around the twelve inch TV to catch the latest episode of General Hospital. *Those were the days.* Now she never watched daytime TV. That is...almost never.

Hunger pains gripped her stomach. She picked up the room service menu, and called the dining room.

"I'll have a grilled cheese sandwich and a Kronenbourg." She usually didn't drink beer. She liked wine and sometimes a cocktail, but for some reason wanted to try it.

Twenty minutes later, she heard a knock on the door.

"Room service," a voice called.

She opened it, directing the young man to set the tray of food on the table. She took the pen he offered and signed the quest ticket.

The beer didn't taste good, yet it relaxed her. She fell asleep lying on the floor in front of the TV. An hour later, the ringing of her cell phone startled her.

"Hello," she said sleepily.

"Melody…Is that you?"

"Yes it's me. Is this Jillian?"

"Yes. I'm in New York visiting Suzette and thought the three of us should get together for lunch and shopping."

"Sounds like fun, but I'll have to take a rain check. I'm in Paris on business." She could have sworn she'd told her friend about the assignment.

"Oh yeah…I forgot about the decorating job there. How's that going?"

"I'm not sure yet. I'll call you later and let you know."

Chapter Thirteen

"Hello," he said into his cell phone without checking the number.

"Mr. Hoffman, this is Officer Boulanger."

A chill ran through his body as a premonition flashed in his mind. Immediately jumping up from the desk chair, he almost fell, and had to sit back down. The four walls began closing around him. As the host of the morning news show talked about the murder rate in Atlanta, he seemed to point his finger directly at him. It took him a few seconds to regain composure as the authoritive voice on the phone continued.

"Your wife has had an accident and she's at American Hospital. We'll need you to come to Paris for questioning as soon as you can make arrangements."

"What happened? Is she alright?" *how did that bitch survive the lethal dose of pills?* They couldn't track it to him. He'd cleaned up all traces of anything linking him to the crime. He had proof that he'd remained in his hotel room all night long. He'd used his "Paris Id" when checking in, and he'd called the front desk several times, once to request a wake-up call and twice inquiring about local TV programming. Jake, the front desk clerk had even carried on a ten-minute phone conversation with him. They'd talked about the weather there in Connecticut and finally he'd told Jake he was going to bed and asked for the wake-up call. The desk clerk thought he was in his room at the time, which served the purpose of the calls.

"We don't know the facts yet, we'll talk when you get here," the officer said and hung up the phone.

With his nerves shot, he felt as if he'd be sick. His first impulse was to run, he'd done it before. All he had to do is call his man in Haiti and get a new identification. Bruno could arrange any plastic surgery needed to change one's looks. He'd have to lie low for a few weeks to heal, but in the meantime, all his tracks would be erased and new tracks laid. He laughed at the thought, and decided that would be his last alternative.

Calling the airport, he booked a flight to Paris immediately.

"We can get you on our next flight which will leave in two hours," the airline representative informed him. He gave them his credit card number and wrote down the confirmation code on the notepad lying on the desk. It wouldn't take him long to pack, he always kept things close together, just in case he had to get out of somewhere in a hurry. This was one of those times. He wanted to get to Paris and see what had happened. He hoped Felicia didn't remember him being there. One of the side effects of the drug was hallucinations. With all the proof he had of his whereabouts, it should be easy to convince the authorities, especially with Felicia's past history of drug abuse.

****

He dialed Jillian's cell number.

"Hey Teddy Bear, I'm sorry to have to tell you this, but my trip will be extended by a few more days. I'll make it up to you, I promise."

"That's fine dear. I miss you." She hung up the phone, disappointed again. She'd arranged a small welcome home party, thinking he'd be home by the weekend. Now she'd have to postpone it.

Her phone rang again. She picked it up after only one ring to hear her daughter's voice, just what she needed.

"Hi Mom, I thought we could go out to dinner tonight. With the hours I've been working, I've not had the opportunity to entertain you as I planned. Besides, there's someone I want you to meet."

She's right. I've hardly been out of this apartment since coming to the city.

"Is this someone a boy?"

"Yes it is…I've met someone that I like spending time with. His name is Raoul Michelot and he's a painter. He painted the beach murals on my walls."

Jillian admired the murals, but assumed the property owner had them painted. She couldn't believe her daughter had found someone that she liked more than Josh Yancey. She'd loved him since junior high. Jillian always secretly hoped that someday she'd forget him and find someone to love.

"Ok! I'll be ready when you get off work. We'll have dinner at the Del Frisco's, my treat."

"See you then, I love you Mom."

Excited over meeting her daughter's new boyfriend, Jillian picked out something special to wear. It delighted her that Suzette had found happiness. With losing her father at such an early age, she deserved it. Jillian hoped it didn't make her too clinging in her relationships.

48

Chapter Fourteen

Looking at the pictures sitting on the desk in her new office, Suzette thought how blessed she was to have such wonderful people in her life. The picture of her mother and Travis was taken at his condominium on the beach. Looking at her mother's face was like looking into a mirror and seeing herself in a few years. They had the same flawless skin and blue eyes. She'd taken the one of Raoul, standing on the steps of her apartment. It was her favorite picture. He looked a lot like Romain Duras, except more handsome.

Seeing Raoul on a regular basis now, neither of them had mentioned the 'L' word. Feeling certain he would soon, Suzette thought it a good idea to introduce him to her mother. This would be his last year at the university, and then he planned to open a small gallery in the city. He'd confided in her one night after they'd made love in her apartment.

Thinking of Raoul, she smiled with anticipation; she could hardly wait until that evening for her mother to meet him. The only thing she dreaded is not being able to have the man she loved in her bed while her mother visited. *Oh well!* She'd survive. They say "absence makes the heart grow fonder". It'd be much more enjoyable when her mother returned home and the two of them could be together again.

Finding her mother dressed in a pair of white jeans and a yellow silk top that enhanced her golden tan, Suzette felt proud of her, she didn't looked her age at all. Most everyone took them for sisters.

"You look gorgeous Mom."

"Thank you dear, I wanted to look especially nice tonight since I may be meeting my future son-in-law."

"He should be here any minute, he gets out of class at six. I'll change quickly and we can have some tea while waiting for Raoul to arrive."

"Raoul…? Sounds French," Jillian said with a grin.

"Yes he lived in Languedoc until he started college here in New York."

Filling the teapot with water and setting it on the stove, Suzette took two china cups and saucers out of the cabinet over the sink. While waiting for the water to boil, she ran upstairs to change her clothes. She put on jeans and a turtleneck, wanting the night to be casual and relaxed.

Hearing the doorbell ring, Suzette opened it and introduced Raoul to her mother. With his coal black hair and liquid blue eyes, he was as handsome as any man she'd ever seen.

"How do you do Madame? You must be Jillian. You are even more beautiful than Suzette expressed," Raoul said, taking Jillian's hand. His English surprised her. He spoke it well for someone living in France since birth.

"bien, merci," she replied. Stumbling in her French, she'd taken the language in high school, but could never speak it well.

"de reim," he said, teasing back with her.

Ok! Let's speak English here, so we can all understand," Suzette said with a laugh, walking back into the room after taking the teacups to the kitchen sink. She'd never taken any foreign languages.

"Before we go, I want to call Travis to check on him. He sounded so forlorn when he called this morning." Jillian took her cell phone into the bedroom for privacy.

Noticing the saddened look on her mother's face when she came from the bedroom, Suzette tried to comfort her.

"He'll see you've called. When he gets time, he'll call you back. Don't worry Mom. He's busy with his work." She put her arm around her mother and guided her out the door, where Raoul had a cab waiting for them.

Getting to Laduree early, they took a choice table by the window. Delicious aromas coming from the bakery brought back childhood memories for Suzette.

"Mom do you remember when Daddy brought us here?"

"Yes dear, but I'm surprised you remember, you were only five."

Jillian and Suzette ordered the Shrimp Scampi with angel hair pasta while Raoul ordered the Prime Porterhouse.

"I'm starving; I've not eaten since early this morning." He crammed his mouth with a huge piece of steak.

For desert they had the macaroons, Suzette and Jillian love them, but Raoul wasn't fond of them, but ate one anyway. The waiter kept the decaf coffee coming and before they realized it, it was almost midnight.

Chapter Fifteen

"I wish the night didn't have to end, but I have an early class, and need to get some sleep," Raoul said.

"I'm sorry too that we have to call it a night, but we can do it again before I leave," Jillian said, following Raoul and Suzette out into the cool September night. She pulled her shawl tighter around her shoulders.

Jillian could see that her daughter cared deeply for Raoul, but could he take Josh's place in her heart? She hoped so.

Arriving at the apartment, Jillian hurried inside, leaving Suzette alone with Raoul to say their goodnights. She wanted to take a shower and go to bed. She hoped to get in touch with Travis the next morning before he got immersed in business. It concerned her that he hadn't returned her call. Maybe he didn't see the missed call on his cell phone. *That has to be it.* Undressing, she headed for the bathroom.

Coming out of the shower, she wondered if Raoul went home or if Suzette slipped him into her bedroom. She giggled, thinking of the times she'd let Travis spend the night with her and wondered if her daughter ever suspected it.

Tossing and turning, Jillian had a fitful night, getting little sleep. She'd not heard from Travis in almost twenty-four hours. Dragging herself out of bed, she went to the kitchen to make coffee, felling as though she could drink the whole pot alone. She poured a large mug full to the brim. Maybe the caffeine would stimulate her brain, giving her the strength to get out and do something…anything, just to get Travis off her mind.

Being alone in Suzette's apartment, no matter how beautiful, only made Jillian's mood worsen. Going from room to room, she tried to find something to tidy up, but her daughter kept her home immaculate. Turning on the TV, she tried to concentrate on what the women of "The View" were saying. However, after only a few minutes she picked up the remote and pushed the power button off. Grabbing her cell phone, without waiting any longer, she hit the speed dial for Travis's cell phone.

"Hello," said a female voice.

Who is this woman answering Travis' phone? There had to be a logical explanation.

"Could I speak to Travis please?"

51

"There's no one here by that name. This is my husband's cell phone, his name is Stephan." The woman sounded so young. *Maybe she's one of Travis' employees.* It hit her like a ton of bricks when she recognized the voice as the one who answered the phone in Paris.

"Who am I speaking with please?" Jillian tried to remain calm.

"This is Felicia."

Jillian hung up the phone.

Dialing Melody's number, Jillian needed someone to confide in. It'd been weeks since they'd talked and even longer since they'd seen each other.

"Hello…who is this?" Melody said sleepily.

"It's me Mel, I know you're still in Paris, but I need desperately to talk to you."

"Hi Jill, I'm glad you called. You wouldn't believe what happened."

"I'm sorry I forgot about the time difference, which explains the sleepiness I heard in your voice, what is it 6 o'clock there?"

"It's 5 o'clock, but that's ok. I need to get up soon anyway."

"Go ahead and tell me what happened." Jillian sat down with a glass of iced tea. Melody lived such an amazing life.

"You won't believe it…it happened so fast. It still feels like a dream…or a nightmare."

"Don't keep me in suspense any longer."

"Ok…let me start at the beginning. I got a call from this young woman who looked me up on line. She recently woke up from a coma, after a year, and decided she wanted to update her apartment. It's one of the most beautiful places I've ever had the opportunity to work on…" she continued.

Imaging the faces Melody made, Jillian smiled. Her friend had a way of rolling her eyes and twisting her lips to describe her story, as if it made it easier to comprehend.

"Anyway…I saved her life! What do you think about that?" Melody laughed one of her deep-throated laughs and went on talking, "I'm waiting now to see if she wants me to do the job or wants to postpone it. They contacted her husband, who was out of town. The police wanted to question him."

"Why do they suspect him when he wasn't there?"

"Felicia said he came home early and left again. However, just a few days before she told me he'd be gone for two weeks. Sounds like she may be hallucinating from all the pills she took."

Felicia…? Is this a coincidence?

"I've got to go now. I'm going to the hospital to check on her and see if her husband has arrived. You know what they say about saving someone's life…you're responsible for them." Letting out another loud laugh, Melody hung up the phone.

Jillian took a pair of jeans and a sweater out of the closet. She had to get out of the apartment for a while, if only to go for a walk.

Heading down Fifty-Fourth Street, she passed by a travel agency. She considered going in and booking a cruise, which would take her mind off things for a while…or would it? She pictured herself surrounded by beautiful people dancing on the deck and romancing under the stars, in the tropical Islands of the Caribbean. She'd love to go there. However…every picture flashing through her mind was of couples looking lovingly into each other's eyes. She felt lonelier than ever, and missed the man she loved. *How foolish. He'll probably call me today.*

Looking at her watch, she suddenly realized she'd left home, hours ago, without eating breakfast. The Famous Oyster Bar, just ahead, served the best lobster bisque. Her mouth watered.

She went inside, took a seat near the window, and ordered the bisque and a glass of raspberry iced tea. Just as she picked up her spoon, her phone rang.

"Hello." Looking at the display, she smiled smugly.

"Hey Teddy Bear, I'm sorry I got tied up and forgot to call you."

"I've been worried sick about you." She didn't tell him about the girl on the phone, knowing he'd have a reasonable explanation. Everything seemed better now that he'd called.

Jillian finished her lunch, paid the check and walked back out into the September sunshine. She felt reassured after talking to Travis and decided to go into one of the shops and find something special for him. With Christmas coming in a few months, she could save it until then.

Finishing her shopping at Persona, Jillian wanted to get home, take her shoes off, and relax. Lying down to rest awhile before dinner, her phone rang.

"Hello," she said, not looking at the display before answering.

"Hi Jill…this is Mel. Just thought I'd call and let you know I'll be flying home tonight. Felicia's husband arrived and he's with her. He is such a sweetheart; there is no way he could have had anything to do with her drug overdose. It'll be late when I arrive, I'll call you tomorrow."

Looking forward to seeing her friend and talking to her of her apprehensions, Jillian felt much better. Lately she'd had so many mixed feelings concerning Travis. Seems he stayed out of town more than home, and the girl answering his cell phone only added to her fear.

Jillian had crazy dreams all night long. In one dream, she and Melody planned her wedding. In another, Travis married someone else and moved to Paris. She woke up several times in a sweat.

The following morning, she called Travis first thing. After having the dream of him and the other woman, she needed reassuring.

"It's only a dream. Would it make you feel better if I rush things up here in Connecticut and hurry home?"

"Stay as long as needed. I'll be fine after hearing your voice." She felt more foolish than ever.

Melody called the next morning while Jillian sat in the kitchen drinking her first cup of coffee.

"Where would you like to have lunch today?"

"Your choice, I'll meet you there."

"How about Chinese…? What's the name of that little place you like?"

"Ming's, I'll be there at noon."

Heading for the bathroom, Jillian wanted a long hot shower after the restless night she'd had. She didn't feel like she'd slept at all.

Considering what to wear, she took her new wool skirt and knee-high boots out of the closet. They'd be perfect to wear on her lunch date with Melody. The boots were a birthday gift from Travis last year. She wondered what he'd give her this year.

Taking one last look at herself in the hall mirror, she gave an approving wink. The skirt fit like a glove and the jacket matched perfectly. Taking out her phone to call a cab, she looked at her watch. She'd have to hurry.

"Ming's Chinese Restaurant 423 Ninth Ave," she said, getting into the cab. She wanted to ask the driver to hurry, but on second thought didn't want him to cause an accident.

Arriving, she found Melody waiting.

"What took you so long? I thought you said you'd be here at noon."

"Sorry the traffic was murder. Have you been waiting long?"

"About fifteen minutes, but it doesn't matter. I ordered the Sesame chicken for both of us. I remembered it used to be your favorite."

Excited about seeing the other, they were too busy playing catch-up to eat. Melody told her friend all about Felicia and her beautiful apartment. Of course, Jillian filled Melody in on all the facts of Suzette's job and new boyfriend.

"I have a great idea. Why don't we go by her office and visit with her? I'd love to see her," Melody said.

"That's a good idea, we can walk there. It's only a few blocks." Jillian hadn't seen her daughter's office and the thought of going there, excited her.

They arrived at Riggs & Straus advertising and asked the reception to direct them to Suzette's office.

"Go down the hall and turn right." The receptionist looked up from her computer, smiling kindly.

"Thank you." Jillian smiled back.

"What a wonderful surprise," Suzette said, getting up from her chair to welcome her mother and Melody. She gave them each a hug. "Have a seat. It's so good to see you Auntie Melody." She'd always called her that.

"This is a gorgeous office and such a spectacular view," Melody said, looking out the window.

"Yes, I'm fortunate to be in here." Suzette sat back down, leaning back in her chair.

"Oh my God, this is my friend Raoul," Melody said, looking at the pictures on the desk. "I met him when he painted murals at the library. It never dawned on me when Jill told me you dated a French guy." Picking up the other photo, Melody took a long hard look at the man with his arm around Jillian. She'd never met Travis, but heard about him. Seems every time they got together he'd gone out of town on business.

"This must be the one and only Travis I've heard so much about. He's as handsome as you said. He reminds me of someone I've seen before, but can't remember who. Maybe someone I've seen in a movie."

It'd been too long since they'd all three been together. Jillian longed for the days gone by before Thomas died. At the time, Melody was recovering from a heartbreaking divorce. Thomas introduced her to her husband, Johnny. Shortly after they fell in love and married.

Melody's phone rang.

"This is Melody," she said, after digging the phone out of her oversized purse. "Are you at home now? I could fly back next week. I have some things to take care of here before I can leave again. See you then." Melody hung up the phone.

"Who was that?" Jillian asked after noticing the puzzled look on Melody's face.

"That was Felicia. She's already home and wants me to come back to do the apartment."

"Are you going back right away?" Jillian asked.

"I'll go next week. I want to spend some time with my husband before leaving again. Speaking of which, I should get home."

After saying their goodbyes, Melody called a cab to take her home while Jillian opted to walk. The few blocks to the apartment would give her the exercise she needed to burn off the calories from lunch.

She kept thinking of the name 'Felicia', how many women named Felicia did she know? Ironic that she'd heard that name twice within two days. It couldn't be the same one. No way, It had to be a coincidence. She laughed at herself for being foolish, sure Travis would explain it when he came home.

Packed and ready to go, Jillian had her bags sitting at the door when Suzette got up the following day.

"When are you coming back again?"

"Instead of me coming back here, why don't you come home for a visit next month?"

"I have my job and my night classes. You can take off work anytime, you're the CEO."

"If Travis goes out of town next month, I'll come back to visit, but you and Raoul should come down for Thanksgiving. We have the extra quest room for him to stay in."

"That would be great Mom. I'll ask him."

"I have to go now, my cab is here. I'll see you in a few weeks," Jillian said, picking up her bags.

Chapter Sixteen

Melody called Felicia to let her know when to expect her.

"That's great! You can meet my husband," Felicia said.

"I'm looking forward to it." The one time Melody met Stephan, he seemed like a great guy. He'd stood by his wife for a year; waiting for her to come out of the coma. Most men would find someone else.

She arrived at the Hoffman apartment and rang the doorbell. A feeling of déjà vu filled her, and she almost turned away. A few minutes passed before Felicia answered the door, still in her pajamas.

"Hi Felicia, did I get you up?"

"No. I'm having my second cup of coffee, would you like to join me?"

"Sure, I could use a good cup of coffee, the java they serve on the plane sucks!"

"You just missed Stephan, but he'll be back for dinner."

"I can hardly wait to meet him."

Looking around the apartment, it amazed Melody that Felicia wanted to redecorate. *Simply Stunning!* It's the only way to describe this apartment, with balcony and views overlooking a gorgeous planted courtyard. The home had a spacious open plan living and dining area, with designer kitchen, beautifully decorated throughout.

Felicia took a cup from the rack, poured hot coffee in it, and handed it to Melody.

"Let's start by looking at some magazines to get some ideas of what theme you want to go with," Melody said.

"I have pictures that I've cut out of decorating magazines. I'll get them for you."

Waiting for Felicia to come back, Melody picked up the photograph of Stephan. *It's amazing how much he looks like the picture of Travis sitting on Suzette's desk.* She'd never seen two people look so much alike. The hair and eyes were the same color, even the dimple in his chin, just like Travis's.

"Here they are." Felicia walked back into the room before Melody could put the picture back on the table.

"Isn't my husband good-looking?"

"Yes he is very handsome. Does he have any relatives in New York?"

"No, he doesn't have any relatives at all, he was an only child and both parents are dead. Why do you ask?"

"He looks so much like my best friends fiancée."

"Well you know what they say, everyone has a twin somewhere." Felicia handed the folder of pictures to Melody.

"Yeah, I've heard that. Not changing the subject, but we'd better get started or we won't get anything done before dinner." Melody took the pictures from Felicia and sat down on the sofa. "Let's get started," she said after looking them over thoroughly.

"Where do you want to start?" Felicia asked, following Melody out the door and into the elevator.

"I thought we'd go to Crate and Barrel, they have a beautiful selection of furniture there. I was thinking something more European. I saw this beautiful hand-hewn dining table; we could replace the heavy one that you now have in your dining room. We'll also stop by the fabric shop and get ideas for new drapes, something soft, maybe tab-tops for a more casual look. Then we can stop at L'Ami Louis for lunch, I'm craving their French fries." Melody licked her lips.

Melody and Felicia laughed and talked as if they'd known each other forever. Anyone seeing them would think they're best friends, or mother and daughter.

They looked at furniture and fabrics until exhaustion took over.

"Let's take a break and have some lunch," Melody said.

"L'Ami Louis' is a great place," Felicia suggested.

"That's one of my favorites."

The restaurant overflowed with hungry tourist and locals. After standing in line, waiting for only a few minutes, the host saw Melody.

"Come this way Mrs. Mendoza." He led them to a small table in the corner.

"Wow! I didn't realize they knew you. I never thought we'd get in here without reservations."

"I eat here a lot when in Paris, which is often. I have lots of clients and my husband and I visit here twice a year. We came here on our honeymoon and fell in love with it."

"It'd be nice if Stephan could come here for dinner with us before you go back to New York."

"We'll have to arrange it."

"What about tonight?"

"That'll be fine with me, but you'd better asked your husband."

Browsing a few more shops after lunch, they looked at wall hangings and linens.

"I'd like to change the colors in the bathroom," Felicia said, looking at towels to buy. She also bought two throw rugs and a shower curtain to match. Looking at dozens of paintings, she didn't like any of them.

"Have you ever thought about murals? I have a friend back home that paints them. His name is Raoul Michelot.

"When could he come here? I love murals."

"He could probably fly right over. He has classes three days a week, but can take them on-line. He charges about five thousand per wall. Of course that doesn't include travel expense." Having spoken with Raoul, earlier in the week, she knew he needed the money.

"Let's call him right away." Felicia's excitement reminded Melody of a child.

"I'll try to get in touch with him tonight from my hotel." Melody wanted to talk to him alone.

"But I thought you were staying at the apartment with Stephan and me."

"Well…being that you've not had much time with your husband since you got out of the hospital, I thought you might want to be alone with him. I can stay at the hotel and come back in the morning. Besides, I have a lot of work to do on the computer." Melody held up the notepad containing the notes she'd taken. Wanting to unwind after the hectic day, she needed to be alone. After covering several miles on foot, she just wanted to sink into a hot bubble bath and have a drink. Felicia, so young, reminded Melody of herself at that age, she seem to never tire.

"Whatever you think is best for you, but could you at least stay and meet Stephan?" Felicia asked in her little girl voice. Melody liked her, but her actions and her voice were beginning to annoy her. *Maybe that's why Stephan stays away so much.* Felicia told her how he traveled most of the time and when he wasn't out of town, he stayed at his office. That may be the reason she took the pills, to get his attention. Melody's thoughts run in all directions. She needed rest.

"Yes I'll do that," Melody said. "Now let's get this stuff home and have a cup of hot tea."

Arriving at the apartment, they put the packages in the closet. As they sat down to have tea, the phone rang. Felicia answered it.

Melody noticed the disappointment on her face.

"What's wrong?"

"Stephan has to work late, he said don't hold dinner for him."

"I'm sorry." Melody tried to comfort her. She thought of the similarities between Travis and Stephan. Many times, she'd been with Jillian waiting for Travis to come home, only to have him call, saying he had to work late.

Knowing it would take her a while to go over all the notes and try to make sense of them, Melody said goodnight around nine. *Maybe Felicia doesn't know what she wants. Maybe she just needs the company of another human being.*

Walking into the hotel room, she flopped down on the bed and kicked off her shoes. She should have known better than to wear the five inch heels to walk the streets of New York. She usually did most of her shopping online, but Felicia didn't have a computer. *How strange is that?* In this day and age, everyone has a computer. Felicia told her she wanted one, but Stephan didn't want her to have one.

****

Not wanting to move, she'd rather lie there and let the feather comforter swallow her up, but she had to get some work done. She looked at the clock, almost six, she could work until she got tired then take a hot bubble bath before going to bed. She needed sleep more than anything else.

Before opening up her laptop, she called down to the lounge and ordered a vodka tonic with a twist of lime. It'd relax her and put her in the mood to work. Spending two weeks off with her husband had made her lazy. *It'd be nice to be a stay-at-home wife.* She giggled at the thought.

Still working at midnight, Melody forgot about dinner and the bubble bath she'd promised herself. Reluctantly she closed her laptop, and pulled the covers back on the bed. She thought about going to the snack machine and getting a bag of chips, but decided she could wait until breakfast. Closing her eyes, she tried to sleep. She'd forgotten to call Raoul. *Oh well.* She could do it first thing in the morning. Right now, she needed rest.

Having it on her mind the next morning, Melody dialed Raoul's number, but remembering it was in the middle of the night in New York, she hung up. She'd have to wait a few hours, giving him time to get up. Calling Felicia, she told her she'd be there by 9:a.m.

"What about Raoul…is he coming?" Felicia asked.

"I've left a voice mail on his machine." Melody lied, not wanting Felicia to know she'd forgotten to call him. She slipped away at noon and called him.

"I need the money. I'll take the next flight out," he said. "I should be there by tonight. See you then."

Chapter Seventeen

"Hi Teddy Bear, just wanted to let you know how much I miss you. The client wants to go fishing while he's in New York, so I'm going to lease a car and take him fishing. Maybe I can get him to sign the contract while we're out there and then fly back home tonight."

"That sounds wonderful! I think Raoul is coming back to finish the apartment today. We're going to buy new furniture and He is staying until it's delivered. I know you'll love it."

"I'm sure I will Honey. Have fun and I'll see you tomorrow. I love you." Hanging up his cell phone, his plan was in action. Now he had to find a place to run the car down the rocks and into the river. Maybe it'd be better to do it after dark.

He lay across the bed. For some reason he could think better lying down. He didn't want to make any mistakes. This would be the start of a new life for him. He'd finally be free to marry Jillian.

Picking up the remote, he turned on the TV, changing the channel to CNN. The weather man told of the rain and flash flooding in the southern states. Water covered many highways and back roads. A new idea dawned.

If he hurried, he could get there before midnight. Watching the rescuers fighting the wind and rain to bring people out in boats, he planned his next move. He picked up the hotel phone and dialed Felicia, it'd be late there, but she always stayed up until one or two o'clock in the morning.

"Hey Honey, sorry to call so late, but something came up and I wanted to let you know. I have to fly to Memphis to get the other partner to sign the papers and then the deal will be done."

"Can't he fly to New York?" He heard the disappointment in her voice.

"It'll only be one more day, I'll fly out of here on the red eye flight…get him to sign first thing in the morning and then take the next flight back to Paris."

Hanging up, he called the airport and booked a flight, he had to get there and drop his wallet in the area where the flooding was happening. When they found it, they'd think he'd drowned and his body washed out into the river, along with the others. This would be easy.

The airports in Memphis closed due to the weather. Landing at the Jackson-Madison County Airport in Jackson, Tennessee, he leased a car to drive the rest of the way. When he finished there, he'd book a flight home in another name.

Feeling under the lining of his brief case, he pulled out a new driver's license and credit card.

"I'd like to reserve a room for two nights. The name is David Shelton," he said to the desk clerk at Hampton Inn.

He returned the documents to a safe place until he needed them again and closed the lid. He'd also called ahead for a car to be waiting for him at the airport, leased under Stephen Hoffman.

Getting closer to Memphis, he could see the traffic backing up. People tried to get in to check on relatives. Police officers stopped people on the road and made them turn around. He had to get in there and leave the car. Pulling off the next exit before the police could flag him to stop he got around them. Getting to the end of the exit, he could see debris floating and street signs bent over by the wind. Turning to the right, he saw the flashing neon sign of an all night pancake house. Water flooded the parking lot and some of the cars floated away. Men in boats tried to rescue people out of their cars. Collapsing under the pressure, a concrete wall caved in, causing the parking lot to sink. Water covered the cars and some lay on their sides, while people in them screamed and tried to get out. This would be the perfect place to leave the car. It was dark and no one would notice if he pulled his car around to the side and let it go under with the rest.

Turning off the headlights, he drove around to the side of the building. Feeling the ground beginning to give, he jumped into the water just as the car tilted onto its side. Screaming for help, people tried to climb into boats and helicopters as they came in to pick up survivors. *I hope I get out of here alive.*

Standing in water above his waist, he swam to reach solid ground. Being away from the blinking neon sign, he lost direction. He felt something to his side and reached to find a large limb. Climbing onto it, he got high enough in the tree to hide until the helicopters were gone, which from the looks and sounds of things would be most of the night.

Always being a good climber, he got to a fork in the tree with three heavy limbs going in different directions. Snuggling deep into the curve and being more exhausted than he realized, he dozed off.

Being soaking wet and the temperature dropping below forty, he awoke almost frozen. At least it was warmer here than in New York, if he'd been there...he'd have frozen to death by now. Relieved he'd thought to grab his over coat out of the car as he jumped free of it, It'd kept some of the rain off him.

Helicopters and rescue boats, still tried to locate people. He could hear people shouting as they pulled drowned bodies out of the devastation. He needed to get out of here before he froze to death. Knowing the interstate was near; he could probably find a motel to get a warm shower and a bed for the night. Shimming down the tree, he jumped onto the hillside next to the road. Raging water covered the interstate below.

The water on the hillside reached his knees, but at least he could walk in it. Making it across the interstate bridge without anyone paying attention to him, he could see a Days Inn on the other side, and he prayed they had a vacancy.

Seeing the 'vacancy sign' flashing as he climbed up the hill to the hotel, he felt relief. Exhaustion, from walking in the water, overtook him and he didn't know if he could make it. It took every bit of strength he had left to climb the four steps to the entrance.

"I need a room please," he said to a pretty young blond behind the front desk.

"Oh my Gosh…How far have you walked? The roads are closed for miles around." She took out a registration card and handed it to him.

"About five miles down the road, I pulled off the expressway and my car stalled."

"It'll be eighty five dollars plus tax."

"I hope you don't mind these wet bills." Taking out a wad of money, he handed her two fifties.

"I'll need to see your driver's license please."

Reaching into his back pocket, pretending to search for his wallet, he smiled apologetically. "I must have lost my wallet as I swam out of my car."

"It's our policy that we have to have a driver's license or a picture Id when paying with cash. However, in this circumstance I can understand how you could have lost it. So putting my job on the line, I'm going to let you slide this time Mr. Shelton. If any problem occurs, I could lose my job. I'm counting on you to be who you say you are."

"You can put your trust in me." He winked, took the key card, and walked up the stairs to the second floor. He could hardly wait to get out of the wet cloths.

The hot water felt wonderful. He would've loved to stay in the shower longer, but exhaustion took over. Drying himself with a huge towel, he fell onto the bed. As soon as his head hit the pillow, he fell into a sound asleep. The next thing he knew someone knocked on the door.

"Housekeeping…," she yelled.

"I'll be out in ten minutes," he yelled back. Looking at the clock on the bedside table, he jumped out of bed. He'd slept for seven hours, which he needed. Taking his clothes off the hangers in the bathroom, where he'd hung them to dry, he dressed quickly.

Sitting down in the lobby, he watched the devastation on the local news while having his first cup of coffee. He saw his rental car and laughed to himself, he'd left everything that linked him to Stephan Hoffman in the car.

He went to the house phone and called a cab. It'd cost him a pretty penny to get to Jackson, but he had to get back to his room there and pick up his identity. He couldn't wait to get home to Jillian.

Most of the water from the night before had drained away, but some back roads remained closed. He hoped he'd not overlooked something that'd link him back to Stephen. He'd left his cell phone and all identification in the car with everything else. He'd pick up another phone when he got back to New York. It'd been hindsight on his part not having one for each identity. He wouldn't make that mistake again.

The cab driver made small talk and asked plenty of questions, but Travis just grunted or nodded his head, pretending to read the newspaper. When the cab pulled up to the hotel, he jumped out, handing the cabbie a hand full of bills.

"Keep the change."

Slipping up the back stairs of the hotel, he took the "do not disturb" sign off the door and went inside. *It's all over. I can relax now.*

He changed clothes, putting the ones he had on in a garbage bag, he'd throw them in the dumpster outside the hotel. He turned on the TV, to CNN, and watched the devastation going on in neighboring towns. Extremely heavy rains and high winds led to massive mudslides. Three tornadoes touched down within a four-hour time span, killing over forty people they knew of. Some drowned that hadn't been identified yet or even found. Hopefully they'd find his wallet in the destruction and consider him one of those bodies not found.

Reaching into his pocket for his cell phone, he forgot he didn't have it. He needed to buy one so he could call Jillian, not wanting his calls traced from the hotel room. He could pick up a prepaid phone at the Wal-Mart nearby.

Walking through the lobby, he greeted the front desk clerk.

"Nice day, isn't it?"

"Good Afternoon, Mr. Shelton. Considering the storms we had yesterday. Memphis got hit hard. The authorities are still finding people drowned, but some washed out into the river. They're dragging for bodies now."

"Yes, I saw it on the news," he said. "Could you give me directions to Wal-Mart?"

"Go to the light; take a right, its one block on the left. You'll see it from the corner."

As he walked the few blocks, he went over the activities of the last couple days, double checking, making sure he hadn't forgotten anything.

Finding the cell phone he wanted, he slid his credit card through the card reader. Not knowing how to put the minutes on it, he asked the cashier for assistance.

"I'll be glad to help you Mr. Shelton." She took the phone, dialed a number and handed it back to him. "It's ready to go, you have a thousand minutes to use before you buy more.

That was easy. Now he needed to call Jillian.

Chapter Eighteen

Surprised to find Travis waiting for her when she got off work, Jillian squealed with joy. She didn't expect him home for another week.

"Oh darling, I've missed you so much," she said, melting into his arms.

"Let's go home and start making wedding plans," He said. "We've waited long enough."

"What? Do you really mean it?"

"Do you want me to get down on my knee on this dirty sidewalk?"

"No, of course not, you've made me the happiest woman on earth." She threw her arms around his neck. She'd wanted this for so long.

"Now let's go home," he said

"Sounds good to me," she said, getting into the cab with him.

"Do you want a big wedding or will City Hall work for you?" he asked her.

"I'd like a small wedding with just my daughter and a few friends attending." She had to have her best friend Melody there; she'd told her all about Travis. Of course, she'd invite her daughter and Raoul. During their last phone conversation, Suzette confided in her how much she cared for the young Frenchman and Jillian hoped he'd make her daughter happy.

"Whatever, you want Teddy Bear is fine with me."

"What about your family? Do you think they'd come?" Jillian asked.

"I haven't spoken to any of them in years. I wouldn't even know how to contact them."

They arrived at Jillian's house, got out of the cab, and went inside. She excused herself to go upstairs and change out of her suit, while he made cocktails. She wanted to call Melody right away and give her the news, but decided to wait until the following day.

Going back downstairs, she found Travis sitting on the sofa with a faraway look in his eyes.

"A penny for your thoughts." She sat down in his lap, nuzzling his neck and chest.

"Just wondering how I've lived so long without you as my wife." He pulled her closer, kissing her passionately.

****

I feel like the luckiest man on earth. He stood, picked Jillian up in his arms, and carried her to bed.

"Where shall we go on our honeymoon?" He put her on the bed gently, lying down next to her.

"I'd love to go back to Paris," she said, rolling over on top of him.

"I thought Turtle Bay Resort in Hawaii; it's nice there this time of year." He couldn't go to Paris now, it'd be too risky.

"I don't care where we go, as long as we're together." She assisted him in taking off his clothes.

"That's what I love about you. You're so flexible." He laughed, thinking of what Felicia would do when she got the news of his disappearance.

****

The call came the following day. Raoul sat at the table, eating the breakfast of hot croissants and coffee that Felicia prepared for them. He'd finished painting the sunroom and planned on flying out of Paris later that day.

"Hello," Felicia said, answering the phone. "What…? Oh no…he can't be…" She began to cry.

"What is it?" Raoul asked getting up to go to her. Putting his arms around her, he held her as she cried uncontrollably.

"They found my husband's wallet in the devastation of the floods in Memphis, Tennessee. He had to fly there to get a contract signed."

"Oh no, I'm sorry. I don't want to leave you alone, is there anyone I can call for you?"

"No, there's no one…my mother and grandmother live three hundred miles away, they never liked him anyway."

"I'll stay as long as you need me to." He liked being back in his home country and had become attached to Felicia. Alone now, she'd needed someone.

"Thank you so much, I'd deeply appreciate it if you could stay a few more days. They haven't found his body, just his wallet. His identification card had our home phone number on it."

She stayed by the phone for the remainder of the day, eating nothing. Raoul feared she'd be sick. Calling Suzette, he explained he'd be staying a few more days in Paris. Not telling her why, he feared she might suspect him of sleeping with Felicia. It'd crossed his mind, but until now he thought he didn't have a chance. Now he might. She'd need a lot of consoling and would be extremely vulnerable.

Calling Melody, to inform her of the situation, he thought she might want to send her condolences. She'd spent several weeks here in Paris and had become quite close to Felicia.

"Does she need me to come there, I can get a flight this evening," Melody offered.

"I'll ask her when she wakes up. She's only been sleeping a short while and needs her rest."

"I understand, just call if you need me."

It amazed him that such a beautiful young girl would live such a friendless existence. She didn't seem to have any interest except this apartment and her husband, Stephan, who, to Raoul, seemed not to care at all. He'd only met him for a short time at his office the first day he arrived in Paris. From what Melody told him, Stephan thought only of his business, leaving Felicia alone most of the time while he traveled around the country. Raoul thought he'd be more willing to spend time with his wife after her being in a coma for a year. He didn't understand. If he had a beautiful wife such as Felicia, he'd spend every minute he could with her.

"How long have I been asleep?" Felicia asked, coming into the kitchen, taking a seat at the counter.

"Not long. Are you alright?" He poured her a cup of coffee from the pot he'd just brewed.

"Yes I'm fine. It's going to take time for me to get over him."

"Yes I agree; its hard losing someone you love." He recalled the death of his father.

Raoul stayed close, comforting Felicia while she cried for her lost husband.

"He's all I've got to live for," she confided in him one night while watching the evening news. They hoped to hear of more bodies found, but after several days, authorities called off the search.

"Are you sure you don't want me to call your mother? I need to get back to school soon." Raoul didn't want to leave her alone and wished he didn't have to. He'd grown accustom to the comforts of the huge apartment, but then on the other hand, his studies suffered.

"I'll be fine by myself. Nina, our housekeeper comes by often to check on me."

"I'll come back during Thanksgiving break if you want me too." He didn't know how he'd explain it to Suzette; she'd asked him to go to her parents for the holidays. When the time came, he lied, telling her his mother became ill and needed him to come home.

Chapter Nineteen

Suzette drove alone to her mother's house for Thanksgiving, disappointed Raoul couldn't be there, but she understood his mother needed him. This was her first holiday since falling in love. She'd dated a few boys in high school, but never thought she'd find anyone who'd make her forget her first love, Josh.

"The turkey smells good. What can I do to help?" she asked, walking into the kitchen.

"Everything is taken care of. Travis should be here any minute. I've got good news to share as soon as he arrives."

The doorbell rang.

"Here he is now." Jillian rushed to let him in.

"I can guess by the smiles on your faces what the good news is."

Before carving the turkey, Travis made the announcement.

"I'm happy for you both," Suzanne said, hugging her mother, then Travis.

"This is the most wonderful Thanksgiving since your father died." Jillian said, before realizing the sadness in her daughter's eyes. I'm sorry Raoul couldn't make it this year dear."

"That's fine, his mother needed him. Hopefully he'll be here for Christmas."

"This is a wonderful meal Teddy Bear," Travis said, having a second piece of pie.

"After I help you clean up, Mom, I'm going riding around town. I may run across some friends, so I don't know when I'll return."

"That's fine dear, go ahead, my fiancée can help with the clean up." She winked at Travis, letting Suzette know they'd be glad for her to leave them alone.

Suzette rode by the pizza place where she used to hang out with friends, hoping some of the gang might be there. She pulled up in front, got out of the car, and walked inside, surprised to find Josh sitting in a booth alone.

"Hi Josh! How are you? Do you mind if I join you?" She sat down in the seat across from him. His good looks still made her heart flutter. Maybe she wasn't completely over him.

"Want to share a pizza?" he asked as the server came to take their order.

"I had dinner about two hours ago, but I'll have a Coke. How was your Thanksgiving?"

"We didn't celebrate the holiday this year. My mother is depressed because she and my dad are divorcing. It takes everything she has in her just to get out of bed in the mornings. When I left the house, she was still in her bedroom with the door locked. My father is living with his twenty-five year old girlfriend. I never thought there was any truth to male menopause, but my father is living proof. My mother told him she'd forgive him if only he'll come home, but he says he loves this girl." Josh hung his head and she saw a tear slide down his cheek before he wiped it away.

"I'm so sorry." She reached across the table, taking his hand. The spark running through her body told her she didn't love Raoul. She still loved the man sitting across the table from her.

"It's ok, we'll survive. Now tell me about living in the city." Josh seemed truly interested.

"How did you know about me moving to the city?"

"Tara told me."

She enjoyed Josh's company, reminiscing old times.

"I heard you're dating a French guy," Josh said, taking her off guard.

"I suppose Tara told you that as well." She looked at her watch. "I have to get home. My mom and Travis are planning on decorating the Christmas tree."

"Sounds like fun, I doubt we'll put up a tree this year or do anything fun at all. I dread going home."

"Then don't go…come home with me. We can play video games after putting up decorations."

"Are you sure your mother won't mind me coming over?"

"She loves having my friends around. Tara usually spends Thanksgiving with us, but she's not coming home from college until Christmas. I just talked to her on the phone a little while ago."

Walking outside, she noticed the new Corvette convertible Josh drove.

"Nice car. I'd love to take it for a drive sometime." She'd always wanted one, but her mother said they were too dangerous.

"I'm sure I can manage that. How long you gonna be home?"

"I'll return home Sunday after church."

They arrived as Travis carried boxes of decorations from the garage.

"I'll give you a hand with that." Josh grabbed a box of lights while Suzette carried a pinecone wreath.

"Would anyone like hot apple cider?" Jillian asked as she carried in a tray of freshly baked sugar cookies.

"Sure!" Josh said, helping himself to a cookie and a mug of cider.

They stood admiring the artificial tree they'd had for years. Suzette noticed the sadness in Josh's eyes when they plugged in the lights.

"Do you want to go upstairs and play video games?" she asked him.

"Would you rather take my car out for a drive now?"

"Sure, that'd be a great way to end a wonderful day." She changed into jeans and a sweater. "We could drive down by the lake. Maybe some of the old crowd will be there."

"Yeah, that's about all there is to do around here." He handed Suzette his car keys and opened the driver's side door for her.

"I love the way this car drives. I'm definitely getting one." She drove slowly at first, but speeded up after driving a few miles.

Some of their friends sat parked at the boat dock. They seemed surprised to see her with Josh. Everyone knew about the big crush she'd had on him since junior high.

"I need to get out and walk off that big dinner you feed me." Josh patted his stomach, stepping out of the car. "Come, go with me."

She put her hand in his. *Am I dreaming?*

Strolling around the lake, they talked about their past and how they looked forward to the future.

"I'll be leaving home in the spring to go to college. I'm looking forward to it, but at the same time I don't want to leave my friends. I'm afraid it won't ever be the same again. "

"Sure it will be, when you come back, the same friends will be here. They'll just be older, that's all."

"But you won't be here." He took her by surprise with the statement.

"No I won't be here, but I'll be in New York working and thinking of my old friends and how much fun we've had growing up together." She noticed a heartrending look on his face.

"What's wrong?"

"I don't want things to change. I wish we were still kids. Can I tell you something without you laughing at me?"

"What is it?" She knew the divorce bothered him, but with all the friends he'd always had, how could he be so sad? He'd been the most popular boy in school and everyone liked him, even the teachers were taken by his charm. All the girls had a crush on him, including her, and now, the old feelings stirred inside her. She didn't even want to think of Raoul now, next to Josh he seemed less significant.

"Promise you won't laugh at me," he said.

"I promise."

"I've always had a crush on you and thought you'd always be here. Now that you're living in the city, it's just not the same here anymore."

"I think I know how you feel." Then it dawned on her what he said.

"What...? You had a crush on me? Why didn't you let me know? I've always had a crush on you too. I never thought you liked me in that way."

"I've always had feelings for you, but didn't realize until you were gone, just how much I really cared."

"Why didn't you let me know? I've always compared everyone to you. No one could ever measure up to you until I met Raoul."

"Do you love him?"

She hesitated before answering his question, not wanting to say the wrong thing and then have to retract it later. Looking into his eyes, she spoke from her heart.

"I thought I did until I saw you again, now I don't know. If only you'd told me how you felt, things would have been different."

"In what way do you mean different? Would you have stayed here instead of moving to the city?"

"I don't know. I have a good job there that could lead to a great career."

"See what I mean, I couldn't have stopped you from going. You and I want different things out of life. I want a wife and children and you want a career."

"Some people have both. My father had a career and a family."

"Yeah mine too, but he's been having an affair for the last five years. I don't want that to happen to me."

Suzette looked at her watch.

"We'd better get home. It's after midnight."

"Would you like to go for a long ride in the country with me tomorrow?" he asked.

"Sure, call me around noon…not before."

That night, she lay awake thinking over the happenings of the day. Just a few months ago, she'd have been the happiest girl in the world to hear Josh say those things. *This has to be the worst case of bad timing.*

He called at exactly noon the next day.

"Hello. Sure I'm ready and waiting," she said, hearing his car pull into the driveway. *That's just like him, always on time.*

"Where are you going dear? Aren't you going to eat before going out?" Jillian called as Suzette ran out the door.

"I'll be back later. Josh and I are taking a ride in the country."

"Josh…?"

They rode around the lake, stopping several times to take pictures of the scenery. She'd forgotten how comical Josh could be. When they stopped for snacks at the little country store, he spoke in an Australian accent. The old couple behind the register asked him how long he'd been in the states. Another time when they stopped at a gas station to fill up the tank, he got in front of the car and danced like Michael Jackson. Everyone around had a good laugh and wanted more. "Josh I've had so much fun with you today and I loved driving your car, sorry my driving scared you. Now I should be getting home, I promised my mother I'd be home by eight to watch a Julia Roberts movie with her."

"Yeah, I should be going home too. I need to check on my mom."

She wished things were better at home for Josh. Maybe Mr. McKeon would soon come to his senses and come back to his wife, or maybe Mrs. McKeon would find someone else to love, as her mother found Travis.

Josh drove her home and walked her to the door.

"Do you mind if I kiss you?" he asked, taking her hand in his and looking into her eyes.

"Just as friends, I told you I'm in a relationship and it wouldn't be fair to him."

When his lips touched hers the old feelings rushed through her and she knew without a doubt she still loved Josh. *What can I tell Raoul? It'll break his heart.*

76

After Josh's kiss, she glowed. Sitting down on the sofa, she picked up the remote and searched the channels for the movie they wanted to watch. Travis sat in the recliner reading a Newsweek, while Jillian prepared the popcorn.

"Am I in time to catch the beginning of the movie?"

"It starts in five minutes; I'll get us a soda." Travis got up and headed for the kitchen.

"Did you have fun riding around with Josh?" Jillian asked.

"Yes Mom. Josh is always lots of fun. Did you know that his parents are divorcing?"

"No! I didn't know it. I should give Connie a call and see if there's anything I can do."

"I know Josh would appreciate it, his dad has moved out and his mother is depressed." Suzette knew her mother and Connie used to be best friends, but through the years had drifted apart.

"Maybe I'll call her tomorrow and invite her to come shopping with me."

"It might not be a good idea to take her shopping for wedding accessories being her husband just left her."

Chapter Twenty

On the flight home, Raoul tried calling Suzette several times, but got no answer. *She said she'd be back the day after Thanksgiving.*

He thought of Felicia. In the days they'd spent alone in the apartment, she'd opened up to him, telling him how her first husband died, and how she'd met Stephan. Raoul wondered if he only wanted her money. He had a bad feeling about Stephan, one he couldn't pin point.

He arrived at the apartment to find Suzette not home. *Where could she be?* Taking his cell phone out of his pocket, he push speed dial for her number.

"Hi Suzette, I just got back to the apartment. My mother is over her illness and I thought I'd better get back to school. Where are you?"

"I'll arrive later tonight. Travis proposed to my mother. She needed my help shopping for her wedding."

"That's wonderful! I'll see you when you get here. Be careful driving." He hung up the phone, walked to the fridge, and took out a beer. *There's probably a game on.* He lay down on the sofa, turning the TV to a ball game.

****

Suzette walked in, closing the door behind her.

"Raoul, there's something we need to talk about," she said, "I've thought about it all the way home."

"Sounds like bad news from the tone of your voice."

"Well I've been doing a lot of thinking and I've decided that we need to be apart for awhile. I'm not sure that I love you."

"I don't expect you to love me…I don't love you either. I thought we were just having fun with each other."

"Just having fun…Is that what we're doing? I think you should go."

He didn't argue, but took her apartment key off his key ring and handed it to her.

"It was fun while it lasted," he said, walking out the door.

Hailing a cab, he gave the driver his address. He hated going back to the small apartment. Maybe he'd call Felicia the following day and suggest that she have another mural painted in the library of her home. He knew she'd take his advice on anything. After all, she'd just paid him twenty thousand dollars for doing three paintings, and thought she'd gotten a good deal. The woman had so much money she didn't know how to spend it. When she turned twenty-five, in only another year, she'd have more. He could finish college in Paris.

****

Suzette took a hot shower, put on a clean nightshirt, and went to bed. She'd dreaded telling Raoul how she felt, but it hadn't upset him in the least. Actually, he seemed to be glad to leave. Tomorrow she'd have his things packed up and shipped over to his apartment. He didn't have much there, just a few clothes and some CDs.

She flopped down on the sofa, flipped the channel to the news, drank a soda and went to bed. She felt good about the outcome of things. She couldn't wait to tell Josh about breaking up with Raoul.

Getting dressed for work the following morning, she hummed, feeling good about going to the office. Thinking of Josh reminded her of his situation. She picked up her phone and dialed her mother's number.

"Mom, have you call Connie yet?"

"Thanks for reminding me. I'll hang up and call her right this minute."

On the way to work, she called Josh.

"I'm glad you called. I had you on my mind," he said.

"Why don't you visit me on your Christmas break? There's plenty to do here in the city."

"I hoped you'd ask. Will you help me do my Christmas shopping?"

"Only if you help me do mine."

The following weeks, they spent hours on the phone each night. She couldn't be any happier.

The day Josh arrived in New York, three day before Christmas; he waited outside her office building until she got off at five o'clock.

"Would you like a ride, Miss?" he asked, standing propped on the car.

"Sure, I never turn down a ride with a good looking man." She smiled sweetly at him, thinking about what lie ahead that evening. She'd loved him for so long and now realized she'd only gotten involved with Raoul on the rebound.

"Are you hungry? I'm starved, where is the best place to eat?" he asked.

"I thought we'd order pizza and watch a movie tonight, being that I'm tired from working all day." She wanted to be alone with him.

"That's fine with me, if you're sure you don't want to go out." He pulled the car into the busy street and headed toward her apartment. It took twenty minutes to drive the few miles, due to traffic. That's why she never drove her car to the office, but always took a cab.

She unlocked the door to her apartment.

"Welcome to my home," she said, taking his arm, leading him inside.

"This is a beautiful place you have here and I love the murals. Did you have them done or were they already here?"

"I had them done when I first rented the apartment."

"Whoever painted them did a great job." Looking closer, at the painting, he saw the signature Raoul Michelot.

"You don't have to worry...I told you it's over between Raoul and me."

"I know, but he made love to you first. I'll always regret it."

"You put the movie in while I get the paper plates. The pizza delivery man should be here any minute." She headed for the kitchen, coming back a few minutes later carrying paper plates, forks and a bottle of cabernet sauvignon.

This is the most wonderful night of my life. Suzette finished off her last glass of wine before Josh carried her to the bedroom.

The next morning they woke up at nine o'clock, but didn't get out of bed until noon. They had a late breakfast of canned fruit and croissants while she talked endlessly, telling him she had some last minute gifts to purchase before going home the following morning.

"We could go shopping and then have lunch downtown. You'll fall in love with the little Italian restaurant. I eat there every chance I get."

"Sounds great to me, let's take a shower and head out." He pulled her into his arms, kissing her.

"You keep that up and we'll never get out of here."

Chapter Twenty-One

Arriving at home, Suzette loaded Josh's arms with gifts. Jillian and Travis, still in their pajamas, ran out to meet them. Suzette had known for a long time they were sleeping together and was glad her mother had finally stopped hiding it.

"It's so nice to be home," Suzette said as she hugged her mother, while Travis helped Josh unload the car. The colorful lights flashing through the layer of snow on the porch resembled a Thomas Kinkade painting.

Sighing loudly, Suzette looked around at all the lights and noticed many new decorations.

"Mom it's beautiful. How did you do it?" She knew her mother would go all out, as she usually did, but this year she'd outdone herself. There were lights outlining the porch and running up the banisters. The giant Santa and elves swayed gently on the roof, making them seem to come to life. Carols, sounding like angels singing, played gently from a speaker mounted on a light post.

"Travis did it," Jillian said as she smiled at him with adoration.

"It's amazing," Josh said as he sat the packages on the porch, returning for another load.

"I didn't realize you had so much stuff to bring." He said to Suzette. She'd been doing Christmas shopping for the last month.

Jillian served hot apple cider as they came in from the cold. Speakers placed strategically around the room gently played "Silent Night" while a fire blazed in the fireplace. In the corner stood a beautiful six foot Christmas tree decorated with red and gold ornaments, presents wrapped to match.

"It reminds me of the Christmas village that I visited as a child," Suzette said picking up and shaking a package.

"No shaking the packages," her mother. "You'll have to wait until after dinner to find out what's in them. After opening gifts tonight, we're meeting some of the other neighbors to go caroling at the convalescent home. The old people will love it. We also have gifts for them."

"But Mom, Josh and I are planning on hooking up with friends," Suzette said.

"You can do that tomorrow. Today is all about family," Jillian said.

"Yes Mother." Suzette knew not to argue when her mother made a decision.

Connie and her friend, Hoyt, arrived bearing gifts and food. Suzette learned from her mother the two had dated in high school.

"I've made my famous candied yams," Connie said, sitting the dish on the counter, while Hoyt put the packages under the tree.

Jillian baked a ham and made cornbread stuffing along with several vegetable dishes including baked corn pudding.

"It's a feast fit for a king," Josh said jokingly as he sampled a bite of the stuffing.

"The best Christmas ever," Jillian said, winking at Connie.

After dinner they opened gifts.

"I love the earrings Josh, but I've told you about spending money on me," Connie said, putting the diamonds studs in her ears.

"You deserve it Mom."

Once everyone else exchanged gifts, Josh gave Suzette a box from the jewelry store in the mall.

Taking the gold bow off and laying it aside, she opened the box.

"I love it!" She held up her hair for him to hook the gold chain around her neck.

"I saw you admiring it," he said.

"But when did you buy it? I stayed beside you the whole time."

"Not when I went to the restroom." He pulled her close, giving her a kiss

"I'll call Tara to see if she and Dillon want to go caroling with us." Suzette picked up her cell phone.

Josh wore a Santa Clause hat when handing out gifts to the old folks. They all wanted to hug him, and some called him Santa. Connie had knitted scarves for some of the men and booties for the women.

"I think we'll make this a tradition in our family from now on," Connie said, watching the seniors open the scarves and booties she'd knitted.

Jillian handed out cookies and musical Christmas cards, while Suzette and Tara gave each resident a bag of fruit.

"We should do this every year," Suzette said.

"Yes, it'll be a new tradition for our new family," Jillian said, tears in her eyes.

****

"I'll miss you." Josh held Suzette's car door open for her.

"I'll miss you to, but I'll be coming back on weekends to help with the wedding."

"I'll see you then. Remember I love you, and I appreciated your mother helping my mom through her rough spot."

"I'm glad Hoyt moved back here, he's a great guy."

"Yeah it seems my mom may be moving on with her life. I hope so."

Chapter Twenty-Two

Suzette drove home every weekend to help her mother and Connie plan for the wedding. But mainly she came home to be with the man she loved. Every Friday and Saturday night, they'd park at the beach, making love in his sports car.

Suzette loved the fact that Travis would be her step-dad. She thanked God for her mother getting married. Until a year ago, it'd only been the two of them. Now they had a family, including Josh, Connie and Hoyt. One big happy family, she loved it.

"I've decided to have the wedding in the dining room," Jillian told Suzette. "We can move furniture around to give room for dancing. I've hired a caterer, and sent invitations to only a few friends. I wanted to invite more, but Travis didn't want a crowd."

"What is he afraid of?"

"I don't know, but he knows how I love being in crowds. Hopefully he'll get over it."

"Did Melody agree to be your Matron of Honor?"

"Yes, speaking of Melody, we have to pick her up at the airport tonight."

****

"Mom, you are the most beautiful bride I've ever seen."Suzette wiped the tears from her eyes, as Jillian dressed for her wedding.

"I wish Johnny could have come with me," Melody said. "If he could have taken off work…he would have. He knows you're the best friend I've ever had."

"It's almost time Mom. Are you ready?" Suzette held her arm out to her mother. She'd walk her down the aisle, giving her into marriage. She hoped soon her mother would give her away…to Josh.

The organ played the wedding march. Suzette kissed her mother.

"I love you Mom."

"I love you too Suzie. Now let's go." She hooked her arm in her daughter's and walked down the stairs, holding on to the banister intertwined with white and yellow roses. Reaching the parlor they heard a commotion coming from the kitchen.

"What the Hell is going on?" Jillian looked horrified at what she heard.

All of a sudden the music stopped and they heard Melody scream.

"YOU LIAR…! I won't let you hurt my friend the way you hurt Felicia."

"Felicia? Where have I heard that name?" Jillian said, "Oh yeah, that's the name of the woman in Paris, the one who'd been in a coma. It's also the name of the woman who answered Travis' phone."

What did Melody mean? What did she know about Felicia? What was going on? Suzette looked at her mother, confusion showed in her eyes.

"What's happening? Has Melody lost it?"

"I don't know." Walking into the kitchen, they saw Melody standing in front of Travis with tears streaming down her face. She had a wild expression in her eyes, her fist clenched. "Melody what are you doing? You're ruining my wedding," Jillian screamed at her friend.

"He's supposed to be dead!" Melody screamed back.

"Stop it… Right now…Stop it!" Jillian said to her friend.

"But Jillian…You don't understand…he already has a wife. Her name is Felicia, and she lives in Paris." Melody's eyes filled with tears.

"Just go." Jillian screamed at Melody. Looking at Travis, her eyes filled with tears. She knew Melody told the truth. Running back up the stairs, she locked the bedroom door before Suzette could reach her.

"Please God, let this be a nightmare," Suzette prayed.

Staying in her room for the next three weeks, she didn't talk to anyone and wouldn't even let her daughter in. Suzette put food and water outside the door, but upon returning, it set there untouched. Finally, taking a screwdriver, she took the knob off the door and went inside.

"Mom, you have to eat and drink something or I'll have to call the doctor."

"I don't want to, I feel as if my life is over. I was such a fool. Why didn't I check it out when she called in Paris? I didn't want it to be true. I knew something wasn't right."

"I'm so sorry Mom."

****

Jillian didn't go back to work, and in spite of Connie's constant attempts to get her friend out of the house, Jillian remained locked in her room at home, knowing she wouldn't love again for a long time…if ever.

Travis' real name turned out to be Randy Stewart, wanted in three countries for investment fraud, mail fraud, and a drug conspiracy charge. When his trial came up, Jillian didn't attend the hearing, but watched some of it on the news. She saw Felicia there and felt sorry for the scared young women. Raoul sat by her side, holding her hand protectively.

On July 20th, in New York, New York, Randy was sentenced to ninety-six months in prison, to be served concurrent with a sentence of one hundred and twenty one months for mail fraud related to the investment fraud scheme. In addition, he was ordered to pay restitution in the amount of 4.3 million dollars to victims of the investment fraud. He pleaded guilty in February to money laundering and mail fraud. During court proceedings and in court documents, Randy admitted that over a period of approximately ten years, he solicited investments through various entities, including Gad Investment Group, known as GIG, for real estate developments.

As part of the scheme, Randy offered five-year bond certificates with return rates of ten to twenty-four percent. To some investors, he represented that the investments were low risk because a real estate lot was collateral. Investor funds were to be used to develop the infrastructure for residential subdivisions, thereby increasing the value of the real estate. Randy admitted he solicited funds before he acquired property for the development, which was to be known as Ocean Ridge Estates, in Ocean City, Maryland.

Further, unbeknownst to investors, there was an eighty percent mortgage on the property, which foreclosed later. Investors were told they could cancel their investments and receive reimbursements at a reduced interest rate; however, Randy failed to pay those who wished to opt out as well as those whose principle and interest reached maturity. Instead, investor funds were used for his own personal use.

Despite these failures, Randy continued to solicit investments through a real estate investment trust known as Best Properties Inc. Within months, those funds had been spent on himself and other expenses unrelated to the investment.

After doing his time in New York, he'd be tried in Paris and probably serve time at La Santé Prison, a prison located in the XIV arrondissement of Paris. After serving his time there, he'd be tried in Mexico and receive another sentence there. Still having an outstanding drug charge in Cuba, he probably wouldn't live long enough to serve it.

86

Chapter Twenty-Three

Broken and ashamed, Jillian hardly went out anymore, regardless of Connie's constant urging. Locking herself in her bedroom, she stayed for days at a time. Melody also called, trying to help Jillian over the heartache, yet nothing they did got her out of the house. She wanted to stay alone in her room, eating only when Suzette made her.

Within a few months, Jillian lost weight, her eyes lost their sparkle, and her skin no longer glowed. Going for days without a shower, her hair hung in greasy strings and she spent days in the same clothes, usually her pajamas.

She didn't know what day it was when Suzette came to visit, only knowing her daughter came frequently.

"Mom, what are you doing sitting here? It's almost dinnertime. Let me help you get in the shower and then we'll go out to eat. I'm starving, aren't you?"

"No. I'm not hungry."

Ignoring her, Suzette pulled her up by the arms. She couldn't have weighed more than ninety pounds, and Suzette could reach around her upper arm with one hand.

"I don't want to go out."

"You have to eat!" Suzette held firm.

"I will eat, but please don't make me go out of the house." Jillian begged.

"Ok, if you promise to take a shower and wash your hair, I'll make dinner for the two of us."

Coming into the kitchen, thirty minutes later, Jillian wore a white robe with a towel wrapped around her head, admitting the hot water made her feel better. It was the first shower she'd had in four days. Sitting down at the table, Suzette spooned macaroni and cheese onto her plate and sprinkled salad dressing on her tossed salad.

"Tomorrow I'm taking you to the city where I can look after you," Suzette said.

"But I don't want to leave home."

"That's too bad. You're not taking care of yourself, so I'll take care of you. I can't quit my job and move here, therefore you'll have to come stay with me. You can come back home when you start doing better. I lost my father; I don't want to lose you too."

"Why would you lose me? I'm only forty-five years old."

"And I want to make sure you make it to your forty-sixth birthday. Don't argue…you're coming with me."

Jillian didn't like it, but knew she'd have to go with her daughter to shut her up. She could stay a few days in the city and then come back home. Knowing Josh sometimes stayed at Suzette's apartment, she didn't want to impose on them. Remembering how it was when Travis was around, and how she wanted to be alone with him. There she was…thinking of him again. She'd tried to erase him from her mind, but couldn't, still loving him, regardless of what'd he done.

Being in New York didn't bring any improvement in Jillian, if anything she'd gotten worse, and still spent most of the time in her room alone. Suzette tried involving her mother in activities with her and Josh, yet nothing seemed to help.

Coming home from work and finding her mother lying unconscious on the floor, was the last straw for Suzette. Feeling for her pulse, finding it faint, she quickly dialed 911.

"Please hurry. It's my Mom, she's unconscious. Come quick."

"Is there a pulse?"

"There is a pulse, but a very faint one."

"Are her pupils dilated?"

"I didn't check. I only checked for a pulse. Please…please…hurry…" The desperation sounded in her voice. She couldn't go on living if anything happened to her mother, the only family she had.

The next few minutes seemed like hours. The paramedics, rushed in, strapped Jillian to a gurney, carried her out of the apartment, and loaded her into an ambulance. Suzette wanted to ride with her, frowning when the technician informed her she'd only be in the way and could ride up front with him.

Upon arriving at the hospital, she jumped out of the ambulance and ran to the back to check on her mother. Seeing the tubes running from her mother's nose and mouth, she gasp loudly, but the Paramedics assured her, Jillian would be in the best of care.

"As soon as they examine her, someone will be out to talk to you," one of the technicians said. His words and kind face comforted Suzette. He looked to be in his thirties. The gentle way he handled the gurney told her he cared about his patients.

Finding a seat next to an elderly couple, she smiled at them as she sat down. They reminded her of her grandparents, and she felt reassured as they smiled back with kind faces. How ironic, she thought. The man, about the same age as her grandfather when he died, looked like her grandfather. The woman had the same soft voice as her grandmother.

"We're waiting on news of our daughter. She had an accident," The woman said.

"I'm waiting for news of my mother. They brought her here in an ambulance."

"Poor child," the old man said, "let us pray with you."

She bowed her head as the old woman took her hand the same way her grandmother used to do when they prayed. Hearing Josh's voice, a good five minutes later, she raised her head and saw the worry in his face.

"The neighbors told me they saw an ambulance take someone out and thought at first you'd been hurt. When they saw you running alongside the gurney, they realized it must be your mother. I got here as soon as possible. Are you alright?"

"Yes. I'm fine. These wonderful people are praying for her." She turned around to introduce the couple to Josh.

"Where did they go? They were sitting right there in those chairs," she said, baffled.

"Who were they?" Josh asked.

"I didn't get their names. They asked if they could pray with me and we started praying. The man had the same soft eyes and the same calming voice as my grandfather, and the woman held my hand in prayer as my grandmother used to do. Where could they have gone?"

"I didn't see anyone. When I walked up, you were sitting there with your eyes closed."

"I know I didn't imagine them being here."

"I'm so sorry this happened. We should have had someone with her," Josh said, changing the subject.

"I never imagined her doing something like this."

"Yeah me either, this seems like something my mother would do, but not yours. Who would have thought it? When we get her home this time, we're not leaving her alone again." Josh seemed concerned and it warmed Suzette's heart. How could she have thought she loved Raoul?

Waiting together for the doctor to come out and give them news of Jillian's condition, Josh held Suzette as she sobbed quietly. *If not for him, what would I do?* She hoped she never had to find out.

When a nurse came to take them back to the doctor's station, Suzette asked about the elderly couple waiting for news of their daughter.

"I'm sorry, but I didn't see anyone that fits that description. We've not had any accident victims in tonight except your mother," the nurse said.

The double doors opened and in walked a tall man wearing a white lab coat. As he neared, they rose to their feet.

"Hello. My name is Dr. Steve Hardin."

"How do you do Dr. Hardin? Is my mother going to be alright?" Suzanne asked before the doctor could say anything else.

"We've pumped her stomach. She should be fine. However, we're concerned with her overall health, and what made her try to take her life.

Suzette now felt the seriousness of the situation concerning her mother's mental state.

"She recently lost a man she loved very much," she said without going into detail.

"Yes, death can do that to us," he said before continuing to question Suzette about her mother's condition. "How is she eating?" He made notes on Jillian's record.

"Not well, I try to get her to eat, but she says she's not hungry. I just thought after a while she'd be all right. I should have been more attentive." She sounded defeated and continued to blame herself, "Why didn't I see this coming? It's all my fault for not paying closer attention to my mother's needs. I was so wrapped up in trying to make it to the top of the corporate ladder; I didn't see that my mother needs me."

"Don't blame yourself. Thank God, you found her in time. A few more hours and she could have been dead. Do you know where she got the pills?"

"No. there are no pills in my apartment, she must have gone out and gotten them from a doctor." *This is definitely a wakeup call.* Her mother needed her.

"Do you think we should hire someone to be with her at all times?" she asked the doctor.

"Yes I do. But most of all she needs friends and family around her."

"Thank you so much Dr. Hardin," Josh said, "we'll make sure she has friends around her."

"Can we see her now?" Suzette asked.

"Yes, I'm sure she'll like that. We'll keep her overnight and you can take her home tomorrow." The doctor ushered them back to Jillian's room.

****

"Where did you get those pills Mom?" Suzette asked, picking her up the following day.

"I found them in one of Travis' suitcases that he'd left at my house. I intended to give them back to him, and put them in my purse. When I changed purses I forgot about the pills, until taking the purse out of the closet just a few days ago. I thought they must be pain pills, because once he told me his back was giving him problems and he'd gotten some pain killers from his doctor. I feel like such a burden to you and Josh. I wanted to end my life."

"How ridiculous..." Suzette said in shock, "You have never been a burden to us. We love you!" Hearing her mother say such a thing, alarmed Suzette and taking Dr Hardin's advice, she talked her mother into going to see a therapist. It wasn't easy, but after arguing for several days, Jillian gave in and promised she'd go.

Chapter Twenty-Four

Doctor Beverly Hathaway introduced Jillian to a group of women who'd all been scammed by men they thought loved them. It took time, but after a few visits, Jillian opened up and shared her story with the others. Afterwards she felt much better. She also realized she no longer loved Travis, and could live without him in her life. Within a few months, she began going out with some of the new friends she'd made in her therapy sessions.

"Mom, why don't you call Melody? She's been calling several times a week." Suzette poured orange juice into two glasses and handed one to Jillian.

"She wants to fix me up with one of her male friends. I'm not ready yet."

"How do you know unless you try? You may like him."

"Ok, I'll make a deal with you. I'll go out with him one time. If I don't like him, you stop badgering me about dating."

"It's a deal," Suzette agreed.

She met Dave Runyon, a friend of Melody's, at a church picnic. Dave grew up in Long Island and moved back to his childhood home town, after retiring from the Navy. At fifty-one, he looked and acted more like thirty something.

Having two children from a previous marriage, he and Jillian had a lot in common, and found it easy to talk. Jillian didn't trust right away, it took a while. She still found herself doubting after six months of dating, yet spent a lot of time at Dave's lake front home. She could see herself spending the rest of her life with him, with only regret, she didn't know him sooner.

Looking back now, it all seemed like a bad dream. She had a hard time digesting the fact that Travis hurt her so bad that she tried to take her own life. What if she'd died and never gotten the chance to know true happiness with Dave?

Packing her bags, she headed for the ocean. Dave informed her he had a special weekend planned for her. Of course, every weekend with him turned out special for her. She adjusted the radio station, listening to Celine Dion as she drove. *Thank you, God for sending me another man to love.* This time she'd done her homework and gotten to know him before getting serious.

Dave's beach house sat upon a ridge overlooking the bay. She saw him, sitting on the patio, waving. A picture of margaritas sat on the table and he wore a swimsuit. She'd brought her bikini as she usually did when spending the weekend with him. Being a strong swimmer, he could swim five miles without stopping. She could never keep up with him and usually turned back after only a mile.

"There's my girl. Are you ready for our swim?"

"As ready as I'll ever be." She laughed, knowing she didn't have to go if she didn't want to. Unlike Travis, Dave considered her feelings, always asking what she wanted to do.

As usual, he left her behind at the mile marker and continued his daily swim. Swimming back to the beach, she'd wait for him on the shore, *a good time to take a nap.*

She lay back on the sun soaked sand, closing her eyes. The song of the sea gulls shortly soothed her to sleep. Being swept away on a cloud, she floated aimlessly as the warm breeze tickled her arms. What sweet joy to go on and on endlessly, floating on air with no worries...no cares, alone in the universe.

Awaking abruptly, she felt herself beings lifted as if she were a feather. Opening her eyes, she saw Travis bending over her.

"Travis, what are you doing here?" She tried focusing her eyes, but with heavy lids could barely hold them open. Feeling as though her limbs were liquid, she had trouble controlling her body. *Where did he come from?* She was alone and all of a sudden, he appeared out of nowhere.

"I've come back for you. We love each other. We belong together."

"No...No...No...go away...leave me alone...I don't love you anymore...please go away...leave me alone."

"Jillian wake up, are you alright?"

She felt someone shaking her and opened her eyes.

"Dave! You saved me." She clung desperately to him, taking in the scent of the ocean.

"Saved you from what? I heard you yelling long before I got to shore. Were you having a bad dream?" He picked her up and carried her toward the house. "Everything is fine now. I have you and I'll never let anything or anyone bother you again. I love you."

"I love you too." She kissed his naked chest, tasting the salt from the water.

He put her down in the hammock on the porch and sat down next to her.

"Tell me about your bad dream." He stroked her sweat-drenched hair from her face.

"I will someday, but right now I just want to forget about it." She smiled up at him.

"Ok, but you know when you're ready I'll be here to listen." He kissed her lightly on the forehead.

"Thank you for understanding." At that moment, she knew she'd met her soul mate.

"Where are we having dinner tonight?" Dave took her by the hand and led her inside.

"Why don't we order in and go to bed early?" She winked to let him know what she meant. She'd never met anyone who made her feel as special as Dave did, not even her dead husband. Funny how just two years ago she said she'd never date anyone else…and here she is madly in love again.

"You talked me into it." He laughed, pulled her into his arms, and kissed her passionately. She returned the kiss with matching ardor.

Six weeks later, they married in a romantic ceremony at his ocean home. After meeting Jillian for the first time, Dave's children began calling her "Mother".

Printed by Books on Demand GmbH, Norderstedt / Germany